CONTENTS

TRANSLATORS' REFACE

We first discovered Patrícia Galvão in 1968 through the Brazilian poets and essayists Haroldo and Augusto de Campos (and later Décio Pignatari), who had largely been responsible for the rediscovery and interpretation of vanguardist works by Oswald de Andrade in the period of Brazil's literary modernism. Patrícia Galvão (known as Pagu), married to Oswald in the early 1930s, was a figure of special fascination to Augusto de Campos for her poetry written in the

1950s under the pseudonym Solange Sohl. The novel she published in 1933, *Parque Industrial,* a title rarely mentioned, attracted the translators' attention as a previously unknown connection to Oswald's avant-garde prose, his Marxist phase, and the early modernization of São Paulo. Our interest in Galvão as a daring and unconventional figure grew when we learned more about her through contacts in Santos with her second husband, Geraldo Ferraz; with composers who had known her there, Willy Correa de Oliveira and Gilberto Mendes; and with her two sons who live in São Paulo, Rudá de Andrade and Geraldo Galvão Ferraz. We are indebted to Randal Johnson for sending us a photocopy in 1977 of the only copy of the novel in the São Paulo Municipal Library. The book was finally republished in 1981, and in the wake of Augusto de Campos's 1982 anthology *Pagu-Vida-Obra,* Patrícia Galvão became widely known and was even celebrated in plays and films.

From first reading we were certain that we wanted to translate Pagu's novel, and with each successive reading we found it more singular and fascinating. It was an extraordinary discovery in many ways. First of all, it was an early, unknown work by Pagu when she was a young militant still associated with Oswald de Andrade. Stylistically, it bridged the years when many writers combined modernist experimentation with themes of social realism. Its treatment of race and class compared favorably with that of proletarian novels of the same period by Jorge Amado but added a valuable urban, feminist perspective that had not been available before. Scenes of raw anarchist and communist propaganda conveyed how deeply Pagu was involved in promoting workers' political consciousness and revolt. Her novel impressed us by recounting the failures of early industrialization through the stories of individual women and by daring to treat issues of abuse of workers, political confrontation, and sexual exploitation, among others. We found the prose engaging because Pagu wrote from her own experiences and point of view, formed both in the immigrant workers' district where she lived and among the social elite she frequented with Oswald. She portrayed city life in short, expressive, simple, and concise scenes. Characters and settings depicted the young author herself and her immediate social world. And the main characters were women. Pagu reported their working, social, and personal lives and circumstances. In our opinion, the novel holds up as an authentic artistic and ideological portrait of its time. It plays a role in the history of the city of São Paulo and offers a woman's first-hand view of the rites of Latin American modernization.

The main difficulties in translating *Industrial Park* come from its complex tone—both documentary and satirical, descriptive and participatory—and its many references to people and places known in São Paulo circa 1930, centered in the factory district of Braz, but forgotten now: film stars, theaters, factories, social clubs, and streets. The novel is in fact a *roman à clef*, in which the modernists and their social world appear in portrait and self-portrait: Oswald de Andrade became the character Alfredo Rocha, and Pagu identified with Otavia, for example. References to events, places, and personalities obscured by time required research and consultation. When we read that some unemployed men worried about being sent by the police to die by the lash on the *mate laranjeira*, we were left to wonder what the connection was between maté tea and orange trees—until we learned that the Laranjeiras were a notorious family in the state of Paraná who owned large maté plantations that kept workers in slave conditions. The word *duco* used to describe an automobile turned out to be a brand of enamel paint. Almost by chance we learned the meaning of the author's cynical reference to plantation wives as 'Migdal countesses' when in conversation a friend identified 'Zwi Migdal' as a ring of corrupt Polish Jews who sent immigrant women to Brazil for prostitution. Linguistic problems ranged from colloquial or slang expressions and usage of the period to the Italo-Paulista dialect widely spoken in immigrant districts. For example, the local trolleys were called 'shrimp' because of their shape and color. Some problems remain unsolved: no one we contacted could identify the expletive *Pamarona!* which Corina's stepfather shouted when he discovered that she was pregnant. We hope our translation of local references will allow readers to enter and savor Pagu's world of São Paulo circa 1930.

Several terms specific to Brazilian culture should be explained here. A common monetary unit used in Brazil before 1942 was the milreis (a thousand *réis*); a much larger unit, the *conto,* is a thousand milreis. Married women are usually addressed as *Dona* followed by the first name; *Seu* is a similar colloquial form of address for men. *Guaraná* is a carbonated soft drink, made from the crushed seeds of the Amazonian vine, whereas *pinga* is a strong liquor distilled from sugarcane. During Carnival celebrations of this period, atomizer sprays containing ether were common in the streets. The *maxixe,* a precursor of the samba, is an urban dance form characterized by a fast binary rhythm, resulting from the fusion of the habanera, the polka, and syncopated African rhythms. A 'banana,' besides a banana, is a well-known obscene gesture of defiance and contempt made by bending one arm and crossing it with the other.

The translators would like to thank Patrícia Galvão's sons, Rudá de Andrade and Geraldo Galvão Ferraz, for their interest in and support of this project. Many readers and specialists offered suggestions and corrections. Augusto and Lygia de Campos generously shared materials on Pagu and solved many of the text's difficulties. Haroldo de Campos, José Mindlin, Jorge Schwartz, Silviano Santiago, Adriano da Gama Kury, and Raúl Antelo kindly offered suggestions on puzzling referential and linguistic problems. Thanks are also due to colleagues Karin Van den Dool, Enylton de Sá Rego, and Lily Litvak for their comments, to Christopher Ballantyne for his provocative essay on Pagu, and to Yale students Kim Hastings, Robert Myers, Alvaro Brito, and Alma Dizon for helpful suggestions and careful proofreading.

MARA LOBO

PARQUE INDUSTRIAL

ROMANCE PROLETARIO

From 'Industrial Statistics of the State of São Paulo'

1930

'The factories increased their capacity for production and worked intensely beginning with the second year of the European conflict, as the statistics indicate. The values jump from 274.147:000$000 in 1915 to 1.611.633:000$000 in 1923. In the following three years, this bustling activity suffered a serious reduction because of the revolutionary movement of 1924 and the great crisis of electric energy. But, in 1927, the figures increase beyond 1.600.000:000$000 and in the years 1928 and 1929 they exceed two million *contos*. The "record" belongs to the year 1928 with the elevated sum of 2.441.436:000$000. Finally, in 1930, the figure drops to 1.897.188:000$000, because of the economic depression that afflicts the whole world and whose repercussion we began to feel in the month of October 1929.'

Aristides do Amaral – Director

THE STATISTICS AND THE HISTORY OF THE HUMAN

STRATUM THAT SUSTAINS THE INDUSTRIAL PARK

OF SÃO PAULO & SPEAKS THE LANGUAGE OF THIS

BOOK, CAN BE FOUND, UNDER THE CAPITALIST RE-

GIME, IN THE JAILS AND IN THE SLUM HOUSES, IN

THE HOSPITALS & IN THE MORGUES.

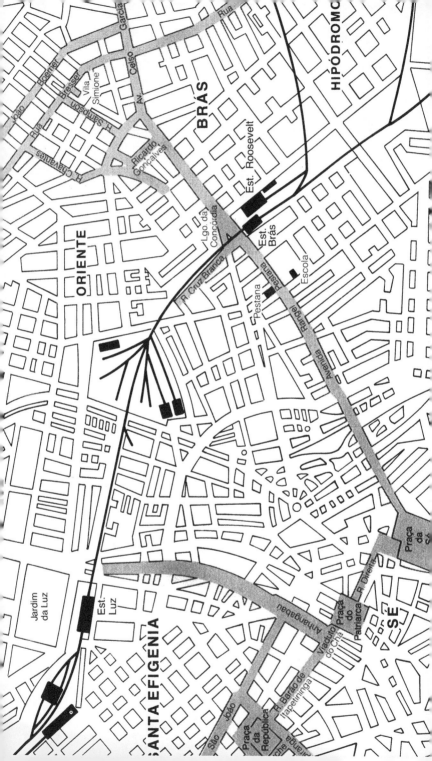

LOOMS

Map (left): The world of the novel extends from the elite Esplanada Hotel on Rua do Arouche (west) and the central Praça da República, across the valley of Anhangabau by viaduct to the commercial district on Rua Barão de Itapetininga and Rua Direita. From the cathedral at Praça da Sé trolleys ran along Avenida Rangel Pestana to the immigrant settlement and factory district of Bras.

São Paulo is the greatest industrial center of South America: The textile workers read on the imperialist crown of the 'shrimp' that rolls by. The Italian girl throws an early morning 'banana' at the trolley. She defends the country.

—Don't believe it! Braz is the greatest!

Through the hundred streets of Braz, the long line of natural sons of society. Natural sons because they are distinguished from others who have had abundant inheritances and every comfort in life. The bourgeoisie always have legitimate sons. Even if their virtuous wives are common adulteresses.

Sampson Street moves full in the direction of the factories. It seems like the worn paving stones are going to break apart.

Colored slippers drag along still sleepy and unhurried on Monday. Wanting to stay behind. Seizing the last small bit of freedom.

The girls tell about the previous evening's dates, squeezing lunches wrapped in brown and green paper.

—I'll only marry a worker!

—Knock on wood! One poor person is enough. Spend my whole life in this shit!

—You think the rich date us seriously? Only to fool around.

—I told Bralio that if it's a fling, I'll tear him apart.

—There's Pedro!

—Is he waiting for you? Then I'll get lost!

The powerful cry of the smokestack envelops the borough. The laggards fly, skirting the factory wall, gritty, long, crowned with spikes. They pant like tired dogs so as not to lose the day's pay. A small red slipper without a sole is abandoned in the gutter. A shoeless foot is cut on the shivers of a milk bottle. A dark girl goes hopping and crying to reach the black door.

The last kick at a rag ball.

The whistle ends in a blast. The machines shake in desperation. The street is sad and deserted. Banana peels. The residue of black vapors vanishing. Blood mixed with milk.

In the great social penitentiary the looms rise and march noisily.

Bruna is sleepy. She had been at a dance until late. She stops and angrily squeezes her burning eyes. She opens her cavitied mouth, yawns. Her coarse hair is powdered with silk.

—Just think! How short Sunday was. . . The rich can sleep all they want.

—Bruna! You'll get hurt. Watch your braids!

It's her companion nearby.

The Shop Manager drifts by, idly, scowling.

—I said I didn't want any chatter around here!

—She could get hurt. . .

—Loafers! That's why nothing gets done! You tramp!

Bruna awakens. The youth lowers his head in disgust. You have to keep your mouth shut!

That's the way it is, in all the proletarian sectors, every day, every week, every year!

In the salons of the rich, lackey poets declaim:
—How lovely is thy loom!

—Let's go to the latrine to talk. The girl asks:
—May I go outside?
—Again?
—I'm taking a laxative.

The walls above the tile mosaic record the laborers' complaints. Each corner is a tabloid of insults against the bosses, managers, foremen, and comrades who sold out. There are ugly names, cartoons, social teachings, fingerprints.

In the dirty latrines the girls spend a joyful minute stolen from the slave labor.

—The Manager said that from now on we can only come two at a time!

—Can you believe it? Did you see how much trash they wrote!

—That's because before, this was the men's latrine!

—But here's a dirty poem!

—How awful! They should erase it. . .

—What's the meaning of this word 'fascism'?

—Dummy! It's that Mussolini thing.

—Not on your life! Pedro said that here in Brazil there's fascism too.

—It's that Mussolini thing, all right.

—When we get off we'll ask. Gee! Time's almost over and I haven't pissed yet!

She straddles the bowl dropping her white cotton pants.

Two other workers arrive, beat on the door hard.

—Now it's 'ar turn!

—Damn! I got a knot in my britches! See if you can undo me!

They leave for the eleven-thirty lunch. They unwrap their bundles fast. Bread with meat and banana. Some girls crumble a boiled egg in their mouths.

Three black girls read the personals in the 'Braz Journal.'

By the ivied iron fence a group of men and women look for shade. They argue. There is an ardent young woman. The others ask her questions.

A young boy is taken aback. No one had ever told him that he was exploited.

—Rosinha, can you tell me what we ought to do?

Rosinha Lituana explains the mechanism of capitalistic exploitation.

—The factory owner steals the largest part of the work day from each worker. That's how he gets rich at our expense!

—Who told you that?

—Are you blind? Don't you see the automobiles of the people who don't work and our poverty?

—You want me to smash his car?

—If you do that alone, you'll go to jail and the boss will

keep riding in another automobile. But fortunately there is a party, the workers' party, that leads the fight for social revolution.

—The lieutenants?

—No. The lieutenants are fascists.

—Then what?

—The Communist Party. . .

Again the streets are tinged with proletarian colors. It's the Factory letting out.

Some girls have boyfriends. Others don't. They're looking. Mothers leave hurriedly for home to find their mistreated children whom no thief would want to steal.

The manager's limousine races, scattering people. A dirty girl smooths the bumper with her scrawny hand.

Rosinha runs a toothless comb through her flying hair. A bunch of kids walk by her side. A sweet young girl wraps brown arms around her waist. It's Matilde, daughter of Céo who started on the streets and is now on stage.

—Why don't you join the union?

Matilde plays with her curls.

—I'm going to enter the Normal School. Momma doesn't want me to work any more.

A rosy-cheeked girl, full of pep, speaks.

—If you only knew Miguetti. . . Whatever he orders done, I do! Don't you agree, Rosinha?

—We'll see him at the meeting, tonight. You need to know who Miguetti is.

NEEDLE-
WORKERS

Barão de Itapetininga Street. Ice cream and phony models at the seamstresses' noon hour.

In front of the Viennense, great velvet display windows where a shawl blends in.

The girls have an hour for lunch. Madame left by automobile with her gigolo.

On the crowded street, blond heads, frizzy heads, simple skirts.

Otavia hurries. She crosses the street between buses, enters an espresso bar, picks up the stained cup, quickly drinks the coffee. Now in a corner, facing a stale sandwich, she leafs through a book without a cover. She takes no notice of the bar's undulating population looking at her.

—Otavia!

—Where've you been, Rosinha! And the factory?

—We exposed the foreman when he tried to break the strike. They fired me. A few days of hunger. . . They called me a delinquent! Son of a bitch!

—Get a sandwich.

—Now I'm at the Italo.

Corina is the last to return to the atelier. A wide belt of oil-cloth burns red against the same old dress as always.

Her mouth satiated with kisses. The bronze of her head saturated with joy is even more bronzed. Her legs rise, with runs in the stockings, out of extraordinary heels.

She wears embers on her cheeks and a new, futurist handkerchief around her neck.

The noise of the sewing machines begins again after lunch. In a room darkened by tapestries, twelve hands are paired with a cut piece of pajamas.

Madame, stiffened by elastics and smeared with mascara, carelessly smokes her cigarette to the amber of the holder. The working women's eyes are like hers. Tinged with purple, but from night work.

—My pajama is for tomorrow. My party is going to be smashingly intimate! I'm going to cause a furor appearing to my guests in pajamas! I'll be the patroness of intimate evenings. Newspapers will have to buzz. The in crowd is going to indulge!

Dazzled by envy of the party she cannot attend, the shop's dressmaker flashes the platinum in her mottled teeth.

A pale young girl answers the call and stammers that it's impossible to finish the order for the next day.

—What did you say? exclaims the seamstress nudging her into the inner workshop. Do you think that I'm going to displease mademoiselle just because of a few lazy tramps? Today there will be overtime until one in the morning.

—I can't stay at night, Madame! Momma is sick. I have to give her medicine!

—You're staying! Your mother won't die waiting a few hours.

—But I have to!

—Nothing doing. If you go, you're out.

The proletarian returns to her place among her co-workers. She shudders at the idea of losing the job that had been so difficult to find.

Madame runs again to accompany her customer, who jumps into an automobile with a mustachioed young man.

The six seamstresses have different eyes. Corina, whose teeth have never seen a dentist, gives a pretty smile, contented. She is the workshop's mulatto. She thinks about love in the roadster that will come to meet her again after work. Otavia works like an automaton. Georgina aspires to a better life. One of them mutters, in a twitching of needle-pricked fingers that crumple the fabric.

—And they say we're not slaves!

Cathedral Square is a clamor. The multitudes that manipulate the comfort of the rich return tired to their hovels.

The bourgeois newspapers cry out the latest scandals through the neglected mouths of tattered boys.

The capitalist 'shrimp' flings open its door to the victim who will shell out another two hundred *réis,* destined for Wall Street.

The streetcar is stuffed. With department store girls. Receptionists. Stock boys. The whole population of the most exploited, of the least exploited. To their slum houses in the immense proletarian city, Braz.

The 'shrimp' halts gasping, continues. Otavia, Rosinha Lituana, Corina, Luiz, Pepe.

Luiz and Pepe are stock boys at the shirt emporium on Direita Street.

Otavia doesn't waste a moment. She reads. It's a book of propaganda. Simple as a child. She crosses her childlike legs in ordinary stockings. Rosinha Lituana shares her companion's revolutionary fervor and gazes around the benches. Corina is the only one isolated, her eyes closed. Her made-up head in a blue beret, she finds the proselytism of others a drag. She thinks life is colossal!

A child sticky with sugar sucks a sweet in a toothless mouth.

The wind makes all the hair on the streetcar fly.

Corina wakes up on Bresser Street. She gets off, smiles at her co-workers, heads for Simione Settlement. There are boys on the corner. Eyes descend, searching for her shapely legs.

Pepe likes Otavia.

—Are you going to the Mafalda Cinema today? It's ladies' day. They're showing Ricardo Bartélmes!

—I can't. I work nights.

—Too bad!

They part in neighboring doorways of João Boemer Street.

—Where's the money, Corina?

—I spent it.

—Florino will catch you.

Corina thinks about her mother's repugnant friend.

—I'm tired of working for a drunkard who's not my father. I have to eat fast and return to the shop.

—There's no dinner.

—And the money from the gramophone?

Florino, drunk and fat, appears at the gateway to the cul de sac. His belly moves, swaying. He shakes his wooden cane. He wants to beat the street urchins who follow him. He misses. The infernal youths want him to fall.

—Drunk! Drunk!

Two grimy hands grab the old mulatto woman's neck. Corina hides the scene with the door. She's accustomed to it. She leaves. Retouching her lipstick, smiling into her purse mirror. She takes the 14.

The street flows by the trolley windows.

—Yes, I'll go! But tomorrow I'll catch a scolding at the shop.

Arnaldo's garçonnière opens its desired secret for her. One more on the Turkish divan.

Also so many delicacies! So many luscious treats for a stomach that burns from hunger. An open bottle. It's so simple. An inexperienced head on the pillows, drowsy. Sexual mouths suck. Legs incite.

Sudden tears and toilette. Contrition, fear, caresses.

Corina finds her lover cold at the farewell.

—Don't tell anyone.

She cries at the shop. The others think it's because of her terrible stepfather.

Rosinha Lituana and Otavia separate at the enormous and bustling door of the Italo-Brazilian Silk Factory.

—*Ciao!*

—Even if we have to die. . .

—What's the difference in dying from bullets or dying from hunger!

IN A SECTOR OF THE CLASS STRUGGLE

—We don't have time to get to know our children!

Meeting of a regional labor union. Women, men, laborers of all ages. All colors. All mentalities. Aware. Unaware. Informers.

Those who look to the union as the only way to satisfy their immediate demands. Those who are attracted by the union bureaucracy. The future men of the revolution. Revolters. Anarchists. Infiltrators.

A table, an old tablecloth. A water jug, cups. A faulty bell. The directorate.

The infiltrators begin sabotaging, interrupting the speakers.

A cook speaks out. He has a strong voice. He doesn't vacillate. He doesn't search for words. They come. Hair falling in his beautiful eyes. Sweaty undershirt, shaking his vigorous hands. They are stained by dozens of onions chopped daily in the rich restaurant where he works.

—We can't get to know our own children! We leave home at six in the morning. They are sleeping. We return at ten. They are sleeping. We don't have vacations. We don't have Sundays to rest!

At the voice of truth, the crowd churns on the hard benches. The whole hall sweats.

—Let's put a stop to this! You asked to talk for five minutes. You've already been talking for half an hour. We'll end up seeing daybreak here!

The crowd turns around. It's the infiltrator Migueti who interrupted.

—We'll see the dawn here! the cook retorts measuredly. We're discussing very important things for our class. They're worth a little lost sleep. How can I sleep knowing that my little ones are hungry? And I who cook so many tidbits for the rich every day!

The infiltrator asks again for the adjournment of the meeting that stretches on excitedly.

—I have to work tomorrow. And all the comrades present too.

The words of a blacksmith beat vigorously on the Assembly:

—Comrade Migueti fights for individual advantage and wants to sacrifice the common good. He's sabotaging the meeting. He keeps us from speaking. He's carrying out a police action against our class interests. On behalf of the bourgeoisie that exploit us! The assembly will decide.

The majority orders the meeting to continue. The laborers know and point out the infiltrators. They are also workers. Corrupted by the bourgeois police, traitors to their class. Of their own interests.

A construction worker shouts:

—We build palaces and live worse than bourgeois dogs. When we're unemployed, we're treated like bums. If we only have a street bench to sleep on, the police arrest us. And ask why we don't move to the interior. They're ready to send us to die by the lash on the Laranjeira family's maté tea plantation!

An aged factory woman cries:

—My mother is dying! I earn fifty milreis a month. The overlord took everything away from me when I left the shop. I have no money for medicine. Not even to eat.

Rosinha Lituana and Otavia are squeezed into one chair. Near them a dark boy flings open his bright eyes. He seems to feel everything that they're saying.

In the city, the theaters are full. The mansions spend on abundant tables. Factory women work for five years to earn the price of a bourgeois dress. They must work their whole lives to buy a cradle.

—All of this is taken from us! Our daily sweat becomes the champagne they throw out!

P U B L I C
INSTRUCTION

Braz Normal School. Pedagogical stronghold of the bourgeoisie. Studies are not very expensive. Parents want their daughters to become teachers, even if that means eating beans, bananas, and cornbread every day.

The large, yellow, dirty building. The gardener José's garden of ants. Eternal janitors. The handsome doorman who studies Law. The dwarf secretary, a poet. The aging schoolmistresses, drying up. The useless spectacles. The ice cream man. The roasted peanuts. Young ladies entering, leaving. Well dressed. Poorly dressed. The well-dressed ones are daughters of Braz's doctors, and Matilde's the daughter of Arruda's 'girl.' Everyone thinks she's pretty. She has a sad smile. Very green eyes. Her thighs showing under a very short jersey. She buys ice cream for all of them. All sorts of snacks! The money show girls earn! But she doesn't tell anyone that she used to work at the Factory.

Malicious tongues slide over the tall sherbets. Bustling breasts ignite their sexualized nipples in a striped sweater, rubbing.

The poor shoe salesman is excited at a distance.

Celia, the chic Portuguese girl, flat as a board, smiles with an enormous mouth at a rich student.

—Stinker! You don't know your place.

—Don't be silly. He looks just like the screen idol José Mojica himself. Especially with the high-collared shirt.

—The other day I met him in Santana with Dirce.

—Ah! Did you know that her father found her in a house of ill repute on Aurora Street? With a married man. . .

—Who doesn't know. That's why she hasn't been coming. They say that he's going to put her in Good Shepherd.

26

—That's why Normal School girls have a reputation. They demoralize us all.

—Oh, go away! She was examined and she's a virgin. She doesn't do any more than you do at Santana Recreation or than I in Santo Amaro.

—But I never went into a room. . .

—Look at Edith's neckline. She comes that way just to show off her breasts in drawing class.

Gallants park at the corners. The director doesn't want to ruin the name of the School with the daily scandal of amorous couples. No man is permitted to stop near the gate. But blue skirts roll up at the intersections.

Eleonora of the Normal School kisses Matilde, who enrolled again. Like a man.

The heavy bell tolls in the doorman's hand.

—Good morning, *Seu* Carlos!

—Good morning, Blondie!

He doesn't call anyone *dona*. The blue and white throng walks through the neglected rose bushes up to the main staircase. Their hands are slow to separate in the corridors.

—Come in. . . Come in. . .

—Just one more ice cream, *Seu* Carlos!

The girls go up in groups, embracing.

—If you could see what a peachy evening at the Tennis Club!

—I didn't have a dress, otherwise I would have gone to the Teyçandaba.

—I went to the Politeama.

—Go on. With that vulgarity!

—Did you see today's Cinearte? It talks about Russian cinema. . .

—Listen! Do you know what communism is?

—I don't know and I don't want to know.

The girls enter. One arrives late. She steps off the trolley and runs. Breasts pointing. A real looker! Very blonde hair. Very straight.

—Well then, Eleonora? Are you really getting married?

—On my graduation day!

The teachers make their entry into the classes after talking a lot about the crisis. Wilted. Repressed. In the midst of so many plump thighs and pretty girls!

—Damn! I can't believe that this stuff is already gone!

—Lend me that sponge?

—Don't use up all the face powder.

—Shall we go to the Coli? Alfredo is paying!

—Then go by yourself!

—Don't be stupid, Matilde. Eleonora will talk and we will eat.

In the schoolgirls' customary sweet shop, Alfredo Rocha, rich boy, kisses his fiancée's hands. He thinks that Eleonora's gluttonous classmates are infinitely funny. He pays. Says good-bye. The car pulls away conspicuously. The girls' envious eyes follow them.

Eleonora's body shivers at the male touch.
—To Penha, André!
The chic car turns toward a starving multitude carrying signs along the proletarian Avenue. "We want bread and work!" They are the unemployed who march in all the streets of the capitalist world.
Alfredo ignores Eleonora as if absorbed. He murmurs.
—Look who's going to take over the earth!

They arrive. A very ugly little house.
—Why are you bringing me here?

She had never intended to give in completely. She would give him everything, except her virginity. That way, he would marry her. She wouldn't be a fool like the others.

Withdrawn, with moist eyes. He still clutches her bruised body.
—Are you crying?
—Of course not.
—You're going to marry a rich man. . .
She doesn't believe in anything anymore. She says nothing.

She went to her small two-story house with garden on Bresser Street. He goes to an expensive apartment that he occupies in the Esplanada Hotel.

Eleonora's father earns six hundred milreis at the Bureau. Not counting the odd jobs. Her mother was brought up in the kitchen of a feudal house, where she had learned her morals, code of honor, and culinary recipes. They dream of a home like theirs for their daughter. Where the wife is a saint and the husband encores midlife passions.

—As long as Nora's not married, I won't rest.

A black woman helps with the housework.

In the sweet peace of her birthday, friends and relatives appear. The school secretary. The godfather congressman. And that animal and moralistic aunt, squeezing her cushions of fat into the green armchair and belching beers.

Eleonora comes in tired, rearranging the legs that had spread.

After the pies, she is obliged to declaim for those present a ballad full of noises by the Paulista poet Pirotti Laqua.

—Your blessing, papa!

—God bless you, my daughter.

Eleonora goes to sleep, thinking. Everything's clear. She won't get him again! The thing's to try to hide it from her parents and find another sucker!

But she didn't have to. Before a justice of the peace Eleonora married the rich heir she aspired to. She is Madame Alfredo Rocha. Now she enters society. With him she passes through the golden doors of the grand bourgeoisie.

There inside, in the isolated citadel of Brazilian high feudalism, in the lair that lives on the distilled sweat of the Industrial Park, there are progressive counts and pastoral princelings married to women smuggled in by the Migdal ring. Capitalists seduce servants. Countesses romantically make love to horse trainers.

—You're going to have your first disappointment. Let's go to Count Sgrimis's party.

—Who is he?

—The Green Count. . . The king of the Industries of Transformation. . .

The bourgeoisie plan mediocre romances. Jokes ooze from the depths of the cushions. They seep between belches of costly champagne. Caviar is crushed by filled teeth.

From the main wall, a tragic eyeless Chirico spies the

nude shoulder that Patou undressed from the hostess's gown.

Dona Finoca, old patroness of new arts, suffers the courting of a half-dozen novices.

—How can I not be a 'communist' if I'm a modern woman?

—The white tuxedos stand erect in the tropical night, paling the topaz cufflinks on fists of silk.

In the gardens, the couples exchange partners. It's the 'cult of life' in the most modern and free house in Brazil. No one sees the Green Count.

Eleonora, contrary to what Alfredo had thought, is amazed. So much intelligence and so much elegance! She is courted. Insistent admirers. Luxury. Sparkling jewels. A punch more delicious than she had ever imagined existed. She becomes angry when Alfredo wants to leave, annoyed.

He climbs in the automobile behind her, shouting:

—I hate these people! These parasites. . . And I'm one of them!

She tells him that all her new friends disapprove of their living at the hotel.

—Lolita Cintra thinks that you have enough money to give me more comfort.

—You don't think the Esplanada is comfortable? Already? Excuse me! I thought I had married a schoolgirl from the Braz Normal School!

—Alfredo! You offend me. . .

—Fine! Let's change the subject.

—She's going to show me a futurist bungalow in Pacaembú. For a couple. . .

—I know. It costs two hundred *contos*! It belongs to Tinoco. . .

—But it's for company, Alfredo! So we can give parties. At Carnival. . .

—At Carnival I'm going to Braz. . .

—I'll never return to Braz. . .

—It's chic! You'll go.

RACIAL
OPIATE

—There's no more tissue paper in any store. I already went to Domingos' and Fernando's. Only if we go to the Avenue.

All the women laborers wear makeup. They spoil their faces rubbing on red paper and spit.

—Let's go to the Avenue. Everyone get moving!

—I'm going to sprinkle face powder on my head. . .

—Do you want to chip in to buy an ether atomizer?

—Not me. My sugar daddy gives me one.

Chairs in the street. Crates. Fat Italian women. God-mothers stretched out in the gutters. The laps of polka-dotted blue aprons with ruffles and peanuts. Big boys suck kilos of mammaries.

Confetti goes from head to foot. From foot to head.

—Look at the gang! Look at the gang! Chiquita! Girls throw themselves like cats clawing the serpentine streamers. Their sexes are burning. Whistles screech at the traffic lights. The bourgeois go by in their cars agreeing that Braz is good at Carnival.

At Colombo's, white, black, or mulatto women, like run-away girls, don't pay to get in.

—Watch out, kids dancing *maxixe!*

A bear sells paper streamers on the running boards of passing cars. Young girls roar hysterically, afraid of the beast.

All the pretty girls are being felt up. Their little brothers chaperone in exchange for candy. In Braz the bourgeoisie search for new and fresh meat.

—What a piece of little Italian!

—Only her figure. Go talk with her. An illiterate.

—For one night no one needs to know how to read.

—I sent a note to that one.

In his brand new Ford, Eleonora alongside Alfredo stiffens up in an expensive Lenci doll costume and shakes all the bracelets on her arm, wanting to return to the Es-planada.

—There are only mulatto boys here!

The lines of automobiles cross, lengthen, carrying the of-ferings of poor young girls, full of palm leaf fans and gathered streamers. Red Pierrots. Harlequins, Domino masks. Unrecognizable costumes.

—Ah! If only I could ride in the procession!

Noisy Chinese girls drink *guaraná* from the bottle, choking and coughing.

Sadistic orchestras incite:

—Give it to her! Give it to her!

That female Pierrot is sniffing ether. She learned how. An immense Bahiana is snoring on the steps.

—Don't look at that guy in the roadster!

—Don't think that I'm going to give up that prize because of you!

—Let's go! Come on!

—I won't. Let me alone!

A stabbing. A scream. Merry widow. A sheet. The crimson red slices disappear inside the white car with bells.

The beaded butterfly, fluttering down with floppy hair, pokes its hard antennae into the puddle of blood.

Carnival goes on. It smothers and deceives the revolt of the exploited. Of the poor. The last five hundred *réis* for the last glass.

—Buddy, will you give me a streamer?

Bresser Street is brightly lighted. Youths with charcoal mustaches glean confetti from the ground.

—Fa-ces masked! Rag-ged ass!

The bands play on cans and shake instruments of beer caps. A Portuguese transvestite eats pistachios in the doorway. A clown who can hardly walk plays with his urine.

The residents of Simeone Settlement are in *Seu* Fernando's bar.

Corina is talking next to an automobile that stopped near the Pharmacy.

—I can't right now, my dear. I have to go to the Terminus Club. Take you along? You're crazy! Yes I love you. Don't be foolish! Wednesday at the same place. Here's twenty milreis.

Everyone comments on the hunk of man and Corina's good luck.

—Just you wait! It's only slumming. God forbid my speaking ill of others. But can't you all see that she's putting on weight?

Corina drags her wooden clogs in the direction of the tenement, without looking up.

There's activity in all the little houses on João Boemer Street. A group of young Sunday girls tell tales with arms linked. They laugh like crazy.

A handsome youth with long white trousers comes in. A yellow blouse. A jockey cap. On his chin, a beauty mark of India ink. It's Pepe. He knocks on number 12.

—Why won't you come to the Almeida Garret? You want to live like an old lady! You can if you want. But you don't want to come along with me!

—I can't go, Pepe.

You're like a contented bourgeois. Your lack of understanding betrays our class. I'm the one who can't turn away from the struggle to join in Carnival.

Pepe says, after a tender silence:

—Marry me. We'll talk to Father Meireles. . .

—Father Meireles will never marry me! I'll belong to the man that my body cries out for. Without the trickery of the church or the justice of the peace. . .

Pepe is incensed.

—You know? I can't put up with a whore!

He leaves. Otavia disappears into the darkened door. Rosinha Lituana, inside, mimeographs manifestos. Otavia begins to fold them.

Pepe digs his nails into his hands. He enters a bar on Celso Garcia Avenue. The table is full of scribblings. A fat woman with fallen breasts. A monstrous soldier's head. Two deformed sex organs without bodies making love. Pepe erases the drawings with spit.

He leaves the organs.

—Bring me *pinga!*

In front, Father Meireles's church. A lot of girls are being felt up on the steps.

Two young Pierrot girls in the bar. In yellow. Cheap satin. Freckled faces sunk in cabbage collars. They eat sweets. Grown-up boys pay.

—I'm getting little breasts!

—I already have pubic hair!

Pretty teeth laugh.

Pepe drowns himself in *pinga*. He's happier. He looks at the jammed church. He starts to think about religion. About the mass he goes to every Sunday. About the mulatto boy who puts out when he doesn't have money for women. The black women in beads. Girls in organdy. He feels like a fool. What's God for, after all? Damn!

He almost leaves without paying. There's a decorated car nearby. A black chauffeur puts on a tire. There are only young men inside.

—Look at that drunk jockey! Let's take him. They call him. Pepe wants to punch them. He falls into the car, held by strong hands.

—He needs cleaning up!

An hour later, the automobile halts in front of a silent mansion on Brasil Avenue.

'Yesterday the police picked up a bruised man stripped of his costume in a gutter of Jardim América. It appears to be a case of someone who became involved in the practice of immoral acts.'

Corina mends, straining her sight.

Why had she been born mulatto? And so pretty! And when she's made up! The damn problem is her color! Why that difference from other women! Her child was his too. And if he turned out this way, with her color of dried roses! Why do blacks have children? Geez! If Florino found out about the pregnancy! She has the urge to tell her mother. She adores the little child that's coming! How big must it be now? Does it already have eyes? And its little hand?

Vomit chokes her smile. She thinks about the next meeting. As always, the brown roadster at Anhangabahú. The perfumed apartment. Her love in impeccable trousers. That she herself removes with slavish care. She likes to nestle between his legs and feel the little noise of his silk undershorts while she's being enjoyed.

She still has those twenty milreis. . . she'll keep them safe. She'll buy a pair of stockings. Hers are full of holes, unwearable. Florino could find it if he searched her. . . She hides the money inside the empty water jug.

She starts to measure the size of her belly in the mirror.

—It's so enormous! Who couldn't see it, my God!

Her mother surprises her. She reacts badly. Then she regrets it.

The old woman sobs into the wash tank.

All of Simione Settlement knows.

—I always said that tramp would end up in a brothel.

Seu Manoel's thirty-two large teeth appear beneath his mustache.

—Man! If it weren't for that belly!

Other women envy her rich romance.

—What about it! Corina's son will have a car and a maid. He's going to live in a mansion. You think she'll take her mother? And Florino?

None other than Florino appears staggering. As always. Fighting with the street scamps.

—Your daughter's been eaten up! Look at that balloon belly. That the wind blows into the air!

Florino doesn't understand. But he storms into the house bellowing. His cane sings.

—*Porco cane!* Whose flirting belly is that! A cry.

—Let me go, you drunk!

Corina expelled, cries in the gutter, surrounded. Some women talk to her. But the children shout, implacable with bourgeois morals.

—Whore!

—Look at her belly!

She spends the night walking. They fool with her. She doesn't know where he lives. He's not at the garçonnière.

Arnaldo. He had never given her another name. She knew the number of his automobile.

Morning carries her to the workshop.

Madame Joaninha shows up in the afternoon.

The young girls buzz with snickers.

—Did you see, Otavia? Corina with a belly! I swear she is!

One of them is going to blab to Madame. The seamstress calls the mulatto. All become aroused. It's a party for the young ladies. No one feels their colleague's disgrace. Even the sewing gets delayed.

—An abortion? Kill my baby?

Her head is inflamed. Her nostrils flare.

—You tramp! Then, get lost. In my atelier, there are young ladies. I can't put whores in with them.

—Where will I go?

—And your man?

She smiles among tears. In a little while, tonight she will meet her lover. She's almost dead of hunger. If only she had brought the money. She had forgotten it in the pitcher. There had been no time for anything.

Otavia drops her sewing.

—Corina, wait for me at the exit!

She's the only one who still speaks to her. Precisely the one who was least her friend. She had always kept her at a distance. Silly!

They meet, Otavia says to her:

—You're coming home with me. Stay there until you find a job or have the child!

—Can I see Arnaldo whenever I want?

—Corina, don't you see who Arnaldo is? He's nothing but a horrible bourgeois! He'll soon have his fill of you! They are always like that. . .

—But we're engaged. . .

—He'll never marry you. He won't have the courage to take a wife outside his class. The only thing he does is seduce girls like you who are unaware of the abyss that separates us from him.

Otavia, overcome with proselytism, keeps on talking. Corina listens, but doesn't believe her and becomes annoyed. She's the only person who takes her in. They arrive together at the little house on João Boemer Street. Rosinha Lituana is at the doorway, in an enormous colored apron.

—Good news, Otavia. I found a place for you at Italo! You can quit the workshop. And earn five milreis more per month! She takes Corina's hand.

—She's coming to live with me, Otavia says. Come by the doorway tonight. Let's go together to the meeting.

Otavia eats the macaroni and bean soup hungrily. It's always the same. But she always finds it tasty.

—Eat! You have to nourish your baby. He'll be one more worker. You need him to be strong!

She leaves. In the street, Rosinha Lituana waits for her with other workers. They disappear at the corner. They're going to work for a better world. Corina leaves later alone.

—If I should arrive late. . .

She arrives early. She sits down on a bench in Anhangabahú. The automobile with new lacquer stops. It's her love.

—You can't today? But I'm homeless!

She tells him how she had left Simeone Settlement.

She refused to have an abortion. Madame had fired her from the job.

He lets a bill fall and shouts speeding off:

—Don't lose it! It's a hundred bucks!

The roadster beeps Corina's illusion.

She was left like a rag in Anhangabahú. Half a dozen chauffeurs comment on her pregnancy and her legs without stockings.

The falling drizzle is heavier than her crying. The large polkadot chintz runs.

It had been just like this for her mother!

The Chá Viaduct shakes under the rare streetcars. Corina wants to die. Die with her baby. She looks back on the agonized trembling of her young co-worker who had committed suicide last year, smashed on the cobblestones of Formosa Street, after her flight. The other's blood, her broken head, crushed bones.

Her clothes rain with the rain. She returns taciturn to the same bench. Searches. She doesn't find the bill that he had thrown.

A joyous band has fun, in the rain. Three men and a woman. On foot. They go by. They invite her as a joke. Corina joins in, goes along. Like a machine. Gets drunk, smokes. Discerns the blond's golden teeth through the smoke. She laughs too. Gets excited. She wants all the males at the same time.

The following day, a flashy guy takes her to a brothel in Braz.

—Dressed like that, no one will want you.

He opens her blouse, tears her brassiere and pushes her toward the windows by the door.

In twenty-five identical houses, in twenty-five identical doors, there are twenty-five identical pathetic women.

She remembers that with the other seamstresses she mocked the women of Ipiranga Street. She feels repugnance, but she cowers. Between tears, she does as the others.

—Hey! Sweetheart! Come here! I'll give you my button. . .

Little by little her erotic vocabulary enlarges.

46

WHERE SURPLUS VALUE IS SPENT

In the other social sector, Eleonora and Lolita go out to see the samples that Madame Joaninha received. They stroll around together every afternoon.

—Try this Chanel! How wonderful, Nora. It was made for you! It's true, Madame, the buckle on my pink Patou came undone. Send for another.

The made-up French lady sells the remainder of the suspect Parisian merchandise to rich ladies of the landed gentry.

—That's all for today. Send it right away. Tomorrow we'll choose the evening wraps.

For the last time Otavia takes a taxi with the 'groom' to deliver three dresses to the Esplanada. Tomorrow she starts at the Factory. Madame didn't care!

—There are so many unemployed women, waiting for openings!

Alfredo Rocha reads Marx and smokes a Partagas in the rich apartment of the downtown hotel. His slippered feet injure the furry cushions. Annoying little dogs. Dolls. Bohemian chic. A little Chinese maid to wait on the couple. The disarray.

—Ming! Bring me tea with kisses.

His blue pajamas glitter and open slightly. The Chinese woman with bangs leaves the cup behind. Obedient. Accustomed. Tiny. She disappears in the cushions. Coldly she receives her boss's kisses. She'll take a new banknote to the fat, paralytic Chinaman on Conde Sarzedas Street.

—Don't worry, Ming. It must be Eleonora. I'll get the door.

—They're Madame's dresses.

—Come in! Madame isn't in. Wait there for a bit. Are you a seamstress? She should arrive any minute!

—I'm an apprentice. . .

Silence.

—What do you think of your profession? Are you happy?

—I am.

—I am rich, but I'm interested in your class. . . in you. . .

She thinks about Corina. All bourgeois are just alike.

—Don't you believe me?

—If I believe. . . But I prefer to leave the dresses.

—I would enjoy talking with you. . .

—I have to work.

—Do you think that I want to abuse a worker? You're mistaken. Personally you don't interest me. . . It's your class. . .

—Of course! We're the ones who give you this luxury!

—You're mistaken. . . This comfort is a burden to me.

Otavia got up, left.

Ming is frightened. Her chest heaves without breasts. Eyes tighten up under the symmetrical bangs.

—You want her. . .

—Where shall we go, Lolita?

—To the bachelors' cocktail party. . .

The garçonnière has a number of antique and futurist rarities. Furniture and silver pieces. Persian and modern carpets. And a little nasal·Victrola with spilled liquids on a dusty harpsichord.

—Lolita! Viva!

—I brought someone.

—Peachy. There are two of us!

They become inebriated and dance.

—I'm not going home tonight!

—Me neither!

—We'll all sleep together. . .

—Little cow. . .

—Leave my thighs alone!

A sexual desperation of break-up and ruin is in the air. The bourgeoisie entertains itself.

PROSTITUTE

On the street of happy women there's a restlessness. A lot of people. A succession of broken men, in wooden sandals, barefoot. Dirty blacks. Adolescents.

—I prefer the hunchback because no one wants her. At least she's clean!

A twenty-year-old, blond worker. Long hair pasted on his forehead. His clothes mended in different colors, counts his nickels.

—Everything goes for the battle! You want a beer, gal?

—Come in!

It's a gambling house. A Spaniard and a very fat lady. A single large room separated by thin partitions. Pleasure comes together in a single moan. The fat lady sells and drinks beers. The males wait their turn by gambling. The pimp bites the red silk of his tie. He smiles into the steamy mirror, admiring his plastered bangs and good teeth.

—This cripple don't do nothin!

The hunchback doesn't answer. An old satin shoe found in some rich trash, cut like a slipper. Hamstrung legs, with veins popping out. A trunk of natural flesh on her bent back. . .

Splattered with paint, a young wall painter comes in hesitantly. Either he satisfies his sex or his stomach.

The quiet hunchback nestles in the used bed.

—Let me see how diseased you are!

He drops with a blow, bruising her hunchback. The youth enjoys her soft flesh, devouring the prostitute's colossal breasts.

—Give me more. I'm not diseased. All of us are!

—I don't have any more.

The two stare at each other, disgusted.

Corina sells herself in another room. The tentacles of a giant black man envelop her body deformed by advanced pregnancy.

—Your big belly turns me off!

52

A hoarse voice guffaws in the room.

—You can even come without money! I'll pay. . .

Sooty eyes give life to an old phonograph. Dried up teats sway in the greasy dessous. Corina opens the door, tired. One more and she'll have the money for her baby's crib.

Soldiers argue in the street. There's drinking and gambling in the bar.

Cruz Branca Street keeps on unburdening the lifeblood of Braz.

—A worker can't even have sex!

An unemployed onanist plays with himself on the corner. A mulatto woman sucks peppermints. She notices the boy rubbing against the wall. Hysterical, with her hands between her legs, she imitates his tragic gesture for the other women, with tremendous cackles.

—If only I could leave this life!

—Sucker! The rich women are worse than we are. We don't hide it. And it's out of need.

—If I had a job, I wouldn't be here, sick like this!

—Money is the pain of the poor.

BIRTH-
ING HOUSES

The ambulance jingles softly on a curve in Frei Caneca Street. It stops in front of the rusty door of the Maternity Hospital. A very white litter, a very brown arm, waving from the civility of the sheet. One more for the indigents' ward. In the vast room, a bunch of identical beds. Many breasts showing. Of all colors. Full, shriveled. A batch of bald, round, numbered little heads.

—Leave my son here. You'll switch him on me.

She doesn't understand that the distinction is made in the birthing houses themselves. The little children of the paying class stay close to their mothers. The indigents prepare their children for the future separation demanded by work. The bourgeois children are nurtured from early on, linked by the economic umbilical cord.

In the indigent ward in the midst of the hardest labor, smiling white nurses comfort the women giving birth, who are now occupying the poor beds they will lie on later.

—Bed 10. Delivery.

A very tall nurse straightens the pillows and greets the new patient.

—Your name?

—Corina. . .

—Corina what?

—That's all.

—Funny! Almost all the indigents have no surname. You've never had a baby?

—No. I'm so tired. . .

—That goes away. You're going to have a beautiful baby!

—Without a father!

—But the mother is going to adore him for them both.

—Arnaldo.

—Is that going to be his name?

—Yes.

Corina suffers horribly.

If only her sweet mother were there. She likes caresses so much. There is no one to encourage her. She calls the nurse.

—Don't leave me! Stay close to me. Stroke my head. That's good!

She shouts unaware. She uncovers herself.

There in the depths of her legs an enormous hole enlarges extraordinarily. She tears, black. It grows larger. Like a gullet. To vomit suddenly something alive, red.

The nurse recoils. The midwife recoils. The doctor stays. A raising of eyebrows announces the surprise. He examines the bloody mass that cries, soiling the covers. Two thin arms reach out for the child.

—Don't let her see it!

—It's a monster. Without skin. And it's alive!

—This woman is rotten. . .

Corina constantly demands her son. Her eyes are blindfolded, the monster's whimpering close to her.

It's that indigent mulatto woman who killed her son!

—Stupid! Just so she wouldn't have to raise him! Tramp! She should die in jail. . .

—Never mind, my dear. See how beautiful our little baby is! How chubby! Look at the dimples. . . How healthy!

—I'm going to give him all my toys. Now I have a real doll. And you have to buy that high carriage. It's the latest style from New York! For him to go strolling in the Avenue park with the nurse.

The jailed women become agitated in the cell.

—Damn! I don't want a crazy woman here!

A puny pimpled woman comes near the door, shouting:

—Thieves! Where can I steal the money to pay the jailer's fee?

Two comment:

—Gee! She's a mulatto! This thin. . . But she's really pretty. . .

—She sure is.

The heavy grating opens, closes. Corina is in jail.

—What are you doing here?

Always the same question for whoever enters. Corina doesn't answer. She sits down in a corner, on a scrap of a red blanket.

—Geez! Get away! Just look where she went to sit. It's teeming with lice.

—What are you doing here?

—I killed my son. . .

No! God!

They draw back. They come closer again.

—I came here because of money. I was hungry. I stole!

—Me too. I killed because the customer wanted to rob me. It was because he picked me up.

—I actually had a full stomach. But I wanted a *manteau!*

—After all, we are all here because of money. Only this sow who killed her son!

No one knows that it was because of money.

The squatting prisoners eternally repeat their simple stories. Small. Identical.

—If only I had a cigarette!

—Here. Only one, eh?

—Thanks.

—Do you have a man?

—I used to. . .

Corina reviews her past romance.

She would still be able to forgive. If he wanted. . . She cries aloud.

—Don't come close! I'll give you disease. If only you could see! My cunt is a hole!

—Look you fool! I'm rotten too! Come eat with me! Geez! Shitty grub! I feel like throwing this slop in the jailer's face. This stinking spaghetti every day. Son of a bitch!

Corina reads a scrap of torn newspaper. Soft, sleepless eyelids. The lice and fleas nest on her slender body. The dirty mat thrown into a corner of the prison. The blue denim of her long skirt. Her shapely legs, barefoot, dark. She looks them over and crosses them, excited, dragging her long toenails along the protrusions of the wall. She feels her firm flesh. So pretty, she'll grow old alone, in prison.

A freckle-faced guard is glued to the bars.

A BOURGEOIS
VACILLATES

Otavia and Rosinha live together now. In the same tenement where Matilde had come shortly before to stay with
her mother in declining health.

The entry of a luxury automobile excites the collective
houses. Eleonora steps out, elegant, constrained.

—Matilde! I got your address. How awful, you living
here. . .

—What do you want? Momma lost her job. She's getting old.

—She's pretty as ever, you idiot! If she wanted to live with me!

—If it weren't for momma. . .

—Right! I can't take her along. . . Will you come to see me often?

—Sure! I didn't know that you wanted. . .

—Silly! I'm the same as ever. You're my closest girl-friend. What do you do here?

—I decided to study. I talk a lot with two neighbors right next door. They recently came here. I know them from the Factory.

—Well now, what can a factory worker talk about? The same nonsense as Alfredo. That wasted time you could be spending with me. Come have lunch tomorrow. . . A juicy kiss, honey.

Alfredo constantly reads and takes notes. Eleonora entertains herself with Xuxuzinho. The perfumed dog licks her manicured nails pleasurably. He prances sexually on the crimson lap of her pajamas.

—Alfred darling. Today you're going to make yourself scarce. Matilde is coming over. I don't want anyone getting in my way. Come back for tea.

—I'll come back tomorrow.

—Even better!

Matilde arrives, pale in her extremely modest outfit. Her

Russian beret hides her tender eyes. Alfredo kisses her hands and leaves immediately.

Ming serves aperitifs.

Her childish little smile disappears little by little with the kisses. Lunch was short. Ming left. Matilde was undressed and loved.

—I'm not going to leave you today. Let's go on a binge tonight. We have to finish these bottles.

The trickling champagne highlights her small bruised virgin breasts.

—Do you like luxury, Matilde?

—From you. . .

—Why didn't you ever want to, when I was in school?

—You didn't have this apartment or these delicious drinks. . .

Eleonora lacerates her lips.

—Alfredo has arrived. . . He'll take you in the automobile.

Matilde got dressed depressed. Her gray billfold is full of money.

—I'll go by myself, Eleonora. Thanks!

Alfredo also went out into the empty Sunday.

He follows her from a distance. He manages to catch the same streetcar. They get off on Silva Teles Street. Braz's morning is in motion. The vegetable lady can't manage the weight of her basket. The banana woman groans her lazy call.

Matilde disappears through the wide doorway of the tenement. Alfredo hurries. He finds her in sobs clinging to a barefoot young girl. He remembers. It's the apprentice seamstress with whom he had spoken at the Esplanada.

—Did you come with him? Did he do something to you?

—No! It wasn't him! Talk to him!

—Not I!

Otavia leaves her, exclaiming:

—He'll be ashamed to talk to my bare feet. . .

Alfredo comes closer. . .

—Don't go to see Eleonora any more, Matilde. . .

—I won't. . .

—Does that girl live here?

—She lives with another girl in number 10.

A bleached blonde appears, in a flowered shift, calling. . .

—Come in, *Seu* Alfredo. Come have coffee. . .

It's Matilde's mother.

DIVID-
ING WALLS

Automobile Club. Inside flies. The high-class Club asks for relief through the decadent pens of its press flunkies. Now it wants to dupe City Hall, selling it the building that the Club couldn't finish. It's the crisis. São Paulo's nascent capitalism turns its feudal and hairy belly up.

Surplus value decreases, torn away by half a dozen fat money grubbers, from the whole population of State workers, through a suction house called the Industrial Park in alliance with the feudal exploitation of Agriculture, under the banking dictatorship of Imperialism.

The richest, the most aristocratic of Clubs, goes under.

In the vast salon, a half-dozen recalcitrants.

—Beastly life!

—There's nothing for us to do! In Brazil there's no place to spend money. Miserable country!

—I didn't even have a single lay this month!

—The girls here are all stupid. There aren't any more virgins. . .

—They're all professionals!

—Look here, I had a little adventure this week, some young ladies whom we accompanied, Saturday afternoon. Remember? The little devil wasn't interested at all. Neither automobile nor money. That night I called Zezé and we broke into her house there on Arouche Street. She lives with the woman who owns the atelier. Just the two alone. . . It was a devil of a fright. They thought it was a burglar. Also Zezé put on a Far West scene, revolver, black bandanna. . . I grabbed the girl in bed. . . As virgin as they come. . .

—And the police?

—Since when did the police ever go after a politician's son?

—The newspapers didn't report. . .

—Of course not. . . The newspapers are buddies.

—Did you give her any money?

—I gave her teeth marks. . .

The commentary continues about cotton trousers, between two whiskies at the bar.

—What about Lolita?

—She's too easy. Rocha's little blonde is really fantastic. But perverted. She only wants women!

—Did Arnaldo wiggle out of it?

—Of course! He swore that the child wasn't his. And the number of the automobile too! What's more, she had come to the Maternity Hospital from the bordello. . . This time he showed up with a spirited little female bull from the South.

—And the woman of mixed blood?

—Jail.

Another character. Gloves. A loud handkerchief.

—Do you want to hear the latest?

—That little mulatto, acting governor, eh?

—Wimpy lieutenant. Never put on a tuxedo. He belongs in our volunteer battalion. High-class women are at least good for that. . . taming important asses! What devils! It's not just for the Prince of Wales!

The great Paulista plantations always have their mares with old pedigrees at the service of the chosen visitor. Very Brazilian. Pioneer stock. Dark. Fair. Plump. Thin. And worse than countesses of the Rotonde. Those became prim and fat after marriage.

There are a half-dozen women, married, divorced, semi-divorced, virgins, un-virgins, syphilitics, semi-syphilitics. But politically very useful. Little bohemians who know Paris. Hysterical. Made to drive unaccustomed military men mad.

They undress to outfit officers in high-class dress livery. They are the cream. The best families! In a knockout, the men order a dozen tuxedos made. They order a cellar of Chianti. They're capable of selling out the regiment for a cigar. And they occupy São Paulo.

Goodbye five percent of our miserable salary! Eighty thousand workers become disillusioned and put quotation marks around the Revolution.

With each passing day Alfredo feels out of place and useless in that poor agonizing wealth.

He crosses the Viaduct, returns to the Esplanada. Also deserted. Almost closing. He goes to drink a solitary whiskey. He enters the prostitute bar that went high class.

He awakens with the bustle of women entering. They are the emancipated, the intellectuals and the feminists that the bourgeoisie of São Paulo produces.

—I've just left Gaston. Marvelous fingers!

—The best coiffeur in the world! Not even in Paris!

—But you were also like a fury!

—Plantation life, my dear!

—The *Evening News* published my interview on the first page. It was horribly typeset. Those idiot newspaper workers. My best sentence left out!

—The lecture is today. But I think it's best to change the meeting time. So that we can come here!

—Do you think Lili Pinto will show up with the same outfit?

—Disgraceful!

—She thinks that evolution is in the masculinity of the apparel.

—But she knows how to make herself interesting.

—If only! Who couldn't become popular that way?

—Is she still with Cassio?

—And with the others.

The barman creates fiery cocktails. The oysters slide down the well-treated throats of the leaders who want to emancipate women with homemade rum and morality.

A matron wearing a tie and huge beads appears, scattering papers.

—Everyone read. The census is finished. We have a large number of working women. Parents now let their daughters be teachers. And work in government offices. . . Oh! But Brazil is so detestable in the heat. Ah! Mon Palais de Glace!

—If you had arrived earlier, we could have visited the Swedish woman scientist. . .

—Ah! My maid delayed me. With excuses of pregnancy. Dizziness. She ran my bath too cold. That's why she's now out in the street!

The German *garçon*, tall and thin, freshens the cocktails. The pale napkin unintentionally thrashes Mlle. Dulcinéa's face. The sharpened tongue of the little virgin absorbs the crystal cherry.

—The vote for women has been achieved! It's a triumph!

—And women workers?

—They are illiterate. Excluded by nature.

The grand hotel's *garçon* smiles meaningfully.

Alfredo as well. He pays. Leaves. Takes the elevator to the third floor.

Eleonora continues her random adventures. She insists on taking everything from life.

The room, carpeted in blue, eternally unstraightened. The sexual moans beating daily in the ears of the servants and commented upon in all the apartments on the floor. She wants to burst her uterus with pleasure.

Alfredo disgusts her for his negligence in dress. She would prefer at least to have him chic as before. She immensely prefers that well-dressed Hungarian with a blond mustache, whom she saw in the hall. He owns a jai alai court. He's a scoundrel. But he's lusted after like a prince.

She comes in behind Alfredo, playing with the puppy.

—Who did you come with?

—With a Dutch lady.

She puts on her pajamas.

Alfredo perceives in his wife the crumbling of intelligence itself. How mediocre she had become!

—We're not alike in anything, Eleonora!

She toys indifferently with a beach hat she had bought.

The Paulista Educational Radio vomits foxtrots from the wall.

Alfredo feels an unspeakable malaise consume him. Everything about the vacuous woman irritates him. Her pajamas, with lace along the thighs to show her nude. The sparklings of her bracelets. Her painted nails. The peppermints. She whispers.

—Your shirt is so disgusting!

Alfredo blanches.

—You are worthy of your dirty friends! I ask only that you don't dine with me that way. In the hotel they notice. . .

Alfredo comes closer:

—Listen, Eleonora. I took you out of a house where at least everyone worked to live. You believed in the comedy of the high circles. You were contaminated. You sank into the mud of this shameless bourgeoisie! Maybe I was responsible. Maybe not. You would have gotten in through any door. Or even by the back way! You would never accept having to work. And today the bourgeoisie can hardly defend itself. Well stay in it. I'm getting out!

PUBLIC
HOUSING

The shared tanks of the communal house are full of clothes and suds. On the grass, a half-dozen men's trousers and some torn nightshirts. Raw hands rub themselves raw. Snotty children, burnished blond, pull on their wet skirts.

—Let go, you little pest! I have to soap all this! These children are only born to exasperate. . .

—Curses! I'll beat you till the Devil says enough!

—The poor shouldn't have children!

—Here comes Didi! Did you see her baby, what a runt!

A deformed black woman appears with her ashen baby. Out of his weak little mouth slips one teat, shriveled, without milk. The sooty apron dries the baby's bleary eyes.

—Poor people can't even be mothers! I dunno how I got this baby! I have to give him to someone, so the poor thing won't die of hunger. If I keep taking care of him how will I find a job? I have to give him up to take care of other people's children! I'll nurse the sons of the rich and I don't know how mine will get by.

No one says anything. They are almost all in the same situation.

They start talking about the seduction of the neighborhood's young girls.

—One who'll soon be lost is Julinha. 'Magine that she goes into the storeroom and lets the boys do this with her little breasts. The other day, they even overheard a conversation. Taliba was in the latrine and heard her ask Pouco-Roupa if he had stuck it all in!

—What the hell! Children can't help but find out. How can anyone hide it if we're all living in the same room? Everyone has to change clothes together. We have to do everything right next to them. Only the rich can have shame because each one has a separate room.

Otavia and Rosinha arrive from work. Didi tries again to squeeze her breast and wipes it in her son's half-opened mouth.

—I brought condensed milk for your baby, Didi!

—Take this tin of marmalade!

The black woman's toothless mouth doesn't even thank her. . .

—And Matilde?

—She's a little shaky, but fine. She never saw that rich girlfriend again. She works on hosiery. She's doing well.

—Have you given her those pamphlets to read?

—She read them. Shall we take her to the meeting today?

The strident voice of the owner knocks at the doors. The whole tenement gives excuses.

—I don't have it!

—For the love of God, wait till tomorrow.

House number 12 is taboo for the tenement's young girls.

Their mothers forbid their daughters to go near. They know that Dona Catita lives there. Many men go in there. D. Catita wears silk pants and ermine slippers. When she goes out in the mornings, with her pajamas tightly squeezing her wide fleshy hips, everyone turns away. D. Catita drags her furry slippers around the dirty ground of the yard.

Yayá is the young deaf maid who washes the clothes and the stained sheets from house 12.

In the moonlight that almost can't be made out, the kids play with hoops.

Far away, in a corner, Violeta feels in the pants of a pleasure-seeking soldier.

The older girls weave large raffia lamps, ruining their fingers on the wires.

The girls' conversation starts off simple, coy. They sit closer together. The talk heats up, grave, confidential. Their little repressed brains expand and they whisper everything that their mothers know they say.

—Are you a woman yet?

A malicious boy tries to overhear.

—Go away! Girls with girls! Boys with boys!

The youth shrieks:

—Beat it, kid!

He goes to play hide-and-seek. The girls start again.

—Do loose women do it just like the married ones?

Words spring out now in a gush:

—I saw my mother once. . .

—What was it like?

—Some women do it with women!

—I don't believe it. They can't. . .

—Yes they can! I read it in a book.

They become frightened. A soft moan close by.

—Con. . . chi. . . ta! Your father's here! Come inside!

The black cornpone seller is surrounded by the girls.

Matilde has a cat on her lap. D. Catita flounces in from an outing, with packages. Otavia appears at the doorway.

A group of women huddle together resting on bundles of firewood near the washtubs.

—My Ambrozina has a good salary, thank God! She's a typist for a gentleman. At the end of the month we'll get out of this hole. Into a decent house. She earns more than my husband. If she didn't need dresses so much. . . But she says that's the way it is. You should see the coat she bought. . .

Ambrozina arrives. Brought in her boss's automobile that stopped at the corner, shapely, belted snugly at the waist by the big buckle of her bright blue raincoat. She noisily kisses her mother, leaving rouge marks on her face. The proud woman shuffles along in a peal of laughter, tripping over her slippers.

—Quickly, mama! Otherwise we'll be late for the Clara Bow movie!

She goes in the house. The grouped women glance at each other.

—I'll bet she's already. . .

—Miguel saw her go into a bad house. . .

—The one I feel sorry for is her mother!

—Sorry for what? You think she doesn't know?

Half the tenement leaves for the Factory.

The smoke dissipates, blackening the whole street, the whole neighborhood.

The brick mansion, with bars on the windows. The whistle escapes from the giant smokestack, freeing all of humanity that drains onto the streets of misery.

A piece of the Factory returns to the tenement.

—No one works tomorrow!
—No one!

—They're ripping the bread from our mouths! We can't allow it! They lowered our wages more! Dogs!

The textile workers foam with proletarian hate. The poor ranks thicken in an unexpected protest in front of the factory. Robust hands and skeletal hands advance on the great industrialist's luxury limousine stopped there. The elegant chauffeur fled. Glass and upholstery crumble in the hands of the avenging masses.

—This gasoline is our blood!

The Colombo Theater, opaque and illuminated, indifferent to empty stomachs, receives Braz's aristocratic petty bourgeoisie that still have money for the cinema.

At the door, the pale enigma of Greta Garbo, in the poorly drawn colors of a poster. Disarrayed hair. Bitter smile. A prostitute feeding the imperialist pimp of America to distract the masses.

But the masses who don't go to the movies stumble over themselves in the square, around the red flag where the hammer and sickle threaten.

Crimson placards incite to revolt. Clumsy but ardent tongues blend in speeches.

Braz awakens.

The revolt is joyful. The strike a party!

—Comrade soldiers! Don't shoot your own brothers! Turn your arms against the officers!

The horsemen's swords resound on the backs and heads of irate workers.

They only have their arms linked to defend themselves.

The strikers swarm around the horses' hoofs. They retreat.

At the darkened factory doorway a pregnant worker complains:

—My husband is being sacrificed. They'll kill him on me! Let's take our husbands away from this strike!

A dirty worker retorts:

—What weakness, comrade! Everyone's struggling now. There is no individual. We're all proletarians!

A group forms.

—Stay calm, Otavia, you can talk later!

—My children have no food!

—It's best to go back to work.

The women support this betrayal.

—They don't understand, Rosinha. . .

—Wait, I'm going to talk. . .

The tiny voice of the revolutionary rises in the flushed faces of the rally.

—Comrades! We can't remain silent in the midst of this struggle! We must be at the side of our men in the streets, as we are when we work in the factory. We have to fight together against the bourgeoisie that drain our health and turn us into human rags! They take from our breast the last drop of milk that belongs to our little ones to live on champagne and parasitism!

At night, we don't even have the strength to warm our children who are left alone the whole day or shut up in filthy rooms without anyone to look after them! We must not weaken the strike with our complaints! We are behind in the rent and even go hungry, while our bosses who do nothing live in luxury and order the police to attack us! But this still will not make us slaves our whole lives! Comrade Julia is unconsciously doing the police's job! She is betraying her companions and her class! She's what's an example of capitalist exploitation! The bourgeoisie have armed lackeys to defend them. If we don't defend our rightful interests, who will run to our aid? The police reaction is an incitement to fight, because it only proves that we are slaves of the bourgeoisie and that the police are on their side! Sixteen of our comrades are in jail. Why? We must demand that they be freed. Comrades! Let's form an iron front against the barbarity of the bourgeoisie who are in the death throes of their regime and therefore resort to violence and terror! We must have faith in the proletarian victory! Let's fight for the strike and for our captives' freedom! Husbands, companions, brothers, and fiancés! For the general strike! Against the bourgeoisie and their armed lackeys!

Shots, rusty swords, poison gases, horses' hoofs. The throng sees the light, in the stampede and the blood.

BRAZ OF THE WORLD

The police investigate. In the chambers, among secrets, are some traitors. Pepe draws near.

—You promised to give me more.

—You were of no use. Tell me who started it. . . The names. . .

—I already told you. Rosinha Lituana. . . The one who spoke at all the meetings. . .

—Idiot! A child lead a crowd to revolt!

—She did!

He nervously picks up the ten milreis that the inspector throws at him. He'll buy a present to make up with Otavia. They haven't seen each other for a month.

Aimless Sunday. On a street in Moóca, Bresser Street, the private automobiles rev for the races. In the Hippodrome curdled with the elegant, betting tickets waste money. Sunny day. Short hair. Multicolored berets. The popular district becomes aristocratic.

Pepe halts at the doorway.

—Why must I be a poor wretch my whole life? Why?

They comment on a jockey's spill.

—So many fall!

Pepe moves away, his brain wreaked with contradictions, grim with miseries. He feels betrayal in all of his veins. It had been his doing that they had carried Rosinha from the tenement in the police wagon. Otavia's calm refusal irritates him. He buys an ice cream on a stick.

Rosinha Lituana disembarks surrounded by recruits in the enormous Immigration presidio.

She had passed through that house ten years before as an immigrant, very young. She had come from Lithuania with her penniless parents. The postwar had made them immigrate like so many people. They were mixed with many others in the great brick house on Visconde de Parnahyba Street. The same as today. Without the gardens and the window bars.

Afterward they had been directed like merchandise to a feudal plantation that had enslaved them to coffee bushes. Even children picked. The peasants didn't say anything. One day they tried to take his wife away. The youngest son of the house desired the Lithuanian woman's thick braids. He was shut up in a barn room. They had managed to escape at night. Rosa remembered their farewell on the road four days later. Her father had said:

—They'll catch us! Flee with our daughter. . .

She had seen her father for the last time, from a field of tall weeds. Hidden and frightened. He had been tied up like a bull and returned to the modern fiefdom. Crossing policed cities!

Later they had reached Braz, two women alone. Poverty. The useless trips to the Agricultural Patronage, where one day an old man threw them out. They stayed in a basement. Her mother died. At twelve years of age she entered the cloth factory. The revolt against the exploiters and assassins. She discovered the union. She understood the class struggle.

From the bars she leans against, she sees the soldiers' mess. At nine, from the other direction, the luxury train to Rio goes by. The Southern Cross. Each compartment costs four hundred milreis for one night. She earned two hundred a month, sometimes less.

It's hard to get to sleep in the strange bed. She remembers her initiation into the proletarian struggle. She had unmasked someone who sold out to the enemy class.

—Yes she was a child! she had shouted to the stilled assembly. But she worked the whole day and the night shift too!

She had passed out so many manifestos! And the meeting had ended with the singing of the International.

She awakens to the presidio's bugle. The narrow cubicle shines in the sun through the bars.

She climbs up to the window and observes the patio. An unarmed squad below does rhythmic exercises. A white soldier rolls up his faded pants and sticks out feminine legs. Cleaning begins. A toothless private stretches out his thick spats for a bootblack.

The lock turns, making noise at the door. She jumps to the ground. She wipes her face with a cloth. It's a gray-haired black who brings her breakfast. Outside the door there's a guard with a loaded gun.

She hears great peals of laughter down below. It's the presidio warden.

They bring her lunch. She distracts herself with the chatter of the soldiers outside.

—This is a time for saving!

—It certainly is! I'm here because I couldn't find work. . .

—I'm serving my Country. . .

She turns from her food. Goes up to the window. Phrases she recognizes float up to her. Lines of party propaganda. Who is it? She can't make out. But she listens.

—Country. . . trickery! If you have no estate you have no state! We're more brothers to Argentine privates than to our officers! War. . . trickery! To defend what? The property of the rich. . .

—That's the truth!

—Those rich that we defend with our lives are nauseated by our presence. . .

—Poor people have no country.

The black comes by under a tray, carrying plates to the officers' room.

In the interrogation, they tell her they're going to expel her.

—You're a foreigner!

But she's never known another country. She had always given her labor to Brazil's rich!

She smiles bitterly. They're going to take her away from Braz forever. . . What does it matter? She had heard it from the very defenders of the social penitentiary:—Poor people have no country!

But leave Braz! To go where? That hurts her like a tremendous injustice. What does it matter! If in all the countries of the threatened capitalist world, there's a Braz. . .

Other men will remain. Other women will remain.

Braz of Brazil. Braz of the whole world.

WHERE THEY TALK ABOUT ROSA LUXEMBURG

Otavia leaves the Dois Rios Colony for political prisoners almost consumptive. A six-month sentence for being a citizen. Alive because she's strong.

The second-class on the night train that takes her back to São Paulo also carries the latest carioca sambas. The preoccupation with the social struggle has invaded popular songs:

All Hail!
All Hail!

This samba's
Going to land in jail.

On the black wooden bench she reads an evening paper from Rio. The first paper she's read after such a long time. Carnival had been regulated. A lot of people collapsed in the streets from hunger. But there was plenty of champagne at the Municipal Theater. She glances over the other pages. 'The Tragic Northeast.' A drought victim, overcome by hunger, killed her little children. She was taken to jail. An immense portrait illustrates a fascist interview. Brazil needs order!

The Ministry of Agriculture at Boa Vista Estate will cost only 16,000 *contos*. The fantastic toilettes of the acting governor's daughter in Petropólis. Begging is on the increase! The Sino-Japanese conflict. Strikes intensify in Spain. In Greece of the poets! In Greece? Who would have thought? World agitation is a fact! Even columnists know it. At the bottom of a page, lost and fearful, a telegram about the building of socialism in the U.S.S.R.

—I see there are more of us, comrades. . .

The union is seething.

—A year's struggle, Otavia! Enough for a lot of proletarians to become disillusioned working for the bourgeoisie. To understand the class struggle. We expelled some intellectuals; others came in. You know one of them. He definitively left the bourgeoisie. Alfredo. . . He's transformed.

But it was hard to change old habits. . . And his taste for the Hotel Esplanada. There he is!

—I already know.

—Otavia. . . you!

He embraces her ineffably.

—You really became a proletarian?

—I gave up two cows. . . the bourgeoisie and Eleonora. . .

Alfredo Rocha laughs in well-chosen poor clothes.

—Tell me about your exile. . .

Alfredo? Could she believe it? Could her companions be wrong?

She'll talk with him all her free hours to see if she can discover a false position, an opportunistic purpose, a shadow of bossism or opportunism. That great bourgeois from the Esplanada!

Everyone tells her that his political line is perfect.

On a cold Sunday, she enters her rented room, bringing a half-dozen yellow flowers picked on the way back from the street market.

Alfredo follows her, in an old overcoat.

Otavia puts on a checkered apron and gets water ready in

a decanter for coffee. Her breasts bounce in her blouse. Alfredo glances at them by accident.

—You still don't believe me, Otavia!

The water murmurs. The aromatic coffee colors the one chipped cup. Alfredo bites quietly into a piece of cornbread. She smiles.

—I will believe one day.

At night, after the job she got at a bakery, Otavia walks through the streets trying to find one or another old companion from the factory. She peeks into the ice cream shops and the bars. School girls pass by licking sherbets. She goes down Joly Street. The proletarian setting hadn't changed. The same Portuguese vendor's produce stand. She used to buy bananas there. On the corner she almost crashes into the giant figure of her companion Alexandre, whom she had met thundering against the bourgeoisie at the union meeting. In a sleeveless striped shirt talking with two foreign workers.

—Hi there, friend!

The four head for a bar. They sit down. The tables are filled with workers.

—This shit never was a revolution!

—As long as Luiz Carlos Prestes doesn't come. . .

Alexandre breaks into the conversation.

—It would amount to the same thing. . .

—How's that?

—The same thing! He would just replay the black comedy that's out there!

—Then who will set it straight?

—Who?

—We the workers! The exploited need to make the revolution happen.

A common worker comments.

—The revolution won't come about because most people are just like me! I confess that I'm afraid of the police. Whoever wants to can go ahead. . .

—They're many like you, shouts Alexandre. But my children who are still young already understand the class struggle!

Alexandre doesn't know how to read or write. But social reality, coming from his mouth, excites the crowds.

—It's the words of one worker to other workers!

The masses galvanize in the full union hall.

—What party should we support, comrades? The parties of the bourgeoisie? No! The P.R.P. or P.D.? No! The lieutenants? No! All workers must come into the Party of the workers!

The dissidents become quiet. The mighty voice dominates, spreads, registers an act of social revolution.

Alexandre's house is near São Jorge Park. He says it's a house. Bourgeois neighbors, chicken coop. His two little creoles, nine and ten years old, weren't baptized but are named Carlos Marx and Frederico Engels. Marcos and Enguis, as their paralytic grandmother calls them from her dirty bed. From the flimsy mattress, made of patches, she sees the soup boil on a stove of kindling wood.

—Fire's almost goin' out!

The boys' mother was lost many years ago under a pile of sacks at the Santista Mill.

—Come see how pretty my poverty is!

Behind the black giant Otavia and Alfredo appear. Almost night.

Poverty yes. But what a revolt inside that poverty.

Carlos Marx didn't sell a single newspaper in order to nail red union manifestos onto posts in the early morning.

The tin plates fill with broth. The black eats out of a big bowl. Alfredo tries to like the simple and poorly prepared food. He feels happy. He doesn't find Brazil abhorrent, as before. He doesn't need to drown his individualistic irritability in any picturesque scenes, neither in the ovens of the Sahara nor in the glacial Arctic Ocean. He wants them to leave him in Braz. Eating that revolutionary food. Without longing for Cairo hotels or French wines.

Carlos Marx and Frederico Engels come running in to tell that the cook's baby right next door was kidnapped. The mother was at work. The six-year-old sister was taking care of her little brother.

—A well-dressed bourgeois lady thought he was cute in his sister's lap. She got out of her automobile and took him. . . Yesterday afternoon.

Alfredo takes an interest, interrogates:

—Did they go to the police. . .

—The father went. But the deputy of Social Order said that the child is better off in the house of the rich!

Alfredo opens an evening paper that he had brought and looks for the report.

—Not here. There's never space to denounce these bourgeois infamies. . . But look at all this about Lindbergh's son. They say that his mother is the most pitiful woman in the world. The new Virgin Mary!

They smoke in silence. Alfredo tosses the paper. In the ashes, the last burning embers. An old cat shakes her burned paws. Frederico Engels studies. Carlos plays with a dark-skinned girl who comes in. Very dark. Endless scratches on her long, bare legs. They argue.

—Is it true, *Seu* Alexandre? I don't believe it. . .

—She said that Rosa Luxemburg never existed. . .

Otavia sits down on the ground with the children.

—Yes she did exist! She was a German proletarian militant killed by the police because she attacked the bourgeoisie. . .

—Is the woman who kidnapped little Neguinho a bourgeoise?

—Of course! Frederico explains, lifting up the top of the book that he's spelling aloud. If she were poor, the police would kill her just like Rosa Luxemburg.

Otavia explains that the bourgeoisie is the same everywhere. Everywhere they order the police to kill the workers. . .

Alexandre laughs. His immense voice breaks in.

—They kill the workers, but the proletariat doesn't die!

PROLETARIAN-IZATION

Matilde had written to Otavia:

'I have to give you a little bad news. Just as you taught me, everything's great for the materialists. They've just fired me from the Factory, without an explanation, without a reason. Because I refused to go to the boss's room. More than ever, comrade, I feel the class struggle. How I am outraged and happy to have this awareness! When the manager put me in the streets, I felt the full reach of my final proletarian-ization, delayed so many times!

'It's fate. It's impossible for the proletarians not to revolt. Now I have felt all the injustice, all the iniquity, all the infamy of the capitalist regime. The one thing I have to do is to fight ferociously against these bourgeois scoundrels. Fight alongside my comrades in slavery. I will leave Campinas day after tomorrow. And I'll look for you the day I arrive.'

Otavia smiles. She wraps herself in a patchwork quilt. She has a book open on the pillow. The candle on the headboard flickers, ruining her eyesight in searching the tiny letters. She doesn't read. She thinks about the vast world in revolt for the class struggle. In the Brazilian sector, combat intensifies, enlarges.

So many people joining in! The scandalous allegiance of the great bourgeois who was Alfredo Rocha. Now, Matilde who had hesitated so many times! The hesitant and even the indifferent are forced to confront the social question. No one is permitted to be disinterested anymore. It's a fight to the death between two irreconcilable classes. The bourgeoisie splinters, divides, crumbles, marches toward the abyss and toward death. The proletariat rises, asserts itself, becomes acculturated. Any militant understands and studies economic questions with the same facility that a bourgeois leafs through a stupid issue of *Femina*.

The bourgeoisie lost its meaning. The Marxist proletariat found its way through all the dangers and fortifies itself for the final assault. While the bourgeois females descend from Higienópolis and the wealthy neighborhoods for orgies in garçonnières and clubs, their humiliated maids in hats and aprons conspire in the kitchens and gardens of the mansions. The exploited masses are fed up and want a better world!

In the shrill workshop, Alfredo takes the great unknown step of his life. He dons the dark shirt that he had always romantically yearned for and that now his ideology and his economic situation authorize and direct.

Red fire drenches his body with laborious and happy sweat. Finally he is a proletarian. He has left the moral filth of the bourgeoisie for good. If Eleonora only knew! Always dazed by alcohol and by the first male she danced with. The typical decadent. How he had deceived himself by marrying her! He had left her half of his fortune. Much was lost in a publishing venture. With the rest, he supported the struggle. As much as Eleonora tumbles through life, heading for catastrophe, the healthy figure of Otavia revives for him the strong companion, pure and enlightened, that he always wanted.

They go into the Mafalda Cinema to see a Russian film based on Gorky. Unreserved seats are in demand. Slowly Alfredo reads the latest international news in a newspaper. At his side, Otavia notices his fleshy lower lip. His half-open shirt reveals a muscular, hairy chest.

An affection passes from the proletarian's pretty eyes to the bowed head of the new worker. The dry bell announces the film.

In the dark, Otavia wants to wrench from each still spectator's head, from each silent arm, an allegiance to the emotional spasms that envelop her. She squeezes Alfredo's hand. But a lot of people don't wait for the end of the showing.

A group of young women go out lamenting loudly the ten cents wasted on a film without love.

They are the unaware who weigh down the proletariat. Impressed by the image of the bourgeois regime, by the fascination of gowns that they can't have but desire. By automobiles of every color, by the rackets and beaches. Fed on the imperialist opium of American films. Slaves tied to capitalist deception.

But in the front row, two young male workers are enthusiastic, absorbed in the proletarian drama being shown. One of them talked so loudly that Otavia could hear every word.

—No one here understands this bombshell!

Groups demonstrate, waving crumpled crimson posters. The smudged ink of the printed bills demands more bread.

And the successive proletarian speakers take charge of the crowd that invades the streets of the factory district with fists raised.

The police advance, fire. A small woman lies on the ground, crying out with her leg shattered. Her blond Lithuanian hair flows smoothly over her sweaty forehead. Resembling Rosinha.

—Comrades!

Imperialism is resisting! Each imperialist sends his opium to deceive our unaware youth. They want to stifle the revolt that leads the exploited to fight. The United States sends cinema. England, soccer. Italy, priests. France, prostitution.

Alfredo smiles, delighted, in the noisy midst of the union.

—Is cunnilingus imperialism?

—Comrades, we need to be more serious. The struggle approaches.

Alfredo, who was making a joke, turns pale. A rustic proletarian denounces him for persistent bourgeois traits.

—A bourgeois will always be a bourgeois.

Otavia appears in the restless circle. She listens.

They leave together. But she says good-bye at the doorway to the Ingleza. Up ahead she sees Pepe barefoot, going in the Mercadinho do Norte. He's more mature, his hair is long.

He doesn't see her. He enters the bar to get something to eat.

A sordid anarchism took hold of the former salesman at the downtown shirt emporium.

From police informer to chronic unemployed to pimp. If only he could break everything. . . smash. . . destroy! If only he could deflower all the single women!

Midnight. He's hardly spotted any women. He goes to have dinner.

Flies crawl on his plate of fish. The shriveled and pinched bread lies upside down on the tablecloth of wine-colored roses. A woman as red as watermelon flesh serves. Her eyes are buried in dense lashes and she wipes her dirty hands on the zephyr apron. Soggy spaghetti steams in front of the customer.

The other waitress, petite and redheaded, carries her apron like a cross on her back. She clinks the boss's nickles in the leather pouch. She laughs a lot to Pepe, sucking on a necklace of large glass beads.

He asks her:

—How much do you earn?

—Forty milreis and one meal.

—Good grub?

—I wish! Leftovers from the pan. A little tiny bit! I'm like a sardine. I weigh forty-one kilos.

She sat down at his table, encouraged.

They call her from another table. The draft beer foam spills from glasses and mouths.

Pepe flirts with a mulatto girl who came in, blotted with bright colors.

—Sit down over here, girl.

Blue with face powder, she shakes great gold hoops in her ears under the shiver of her hair.

The soft voice of the bar breaks out in guffaws.

—I'll buy you a beer. . .

—For my friend too?

Two fair-skinned, fat-assed boys come through the curtained door.

Otavia realizes that she likes Alfredo.

His inconsistencies after all are natural and insignificant. He doesn't represent to her merely a companion in social ideals and struggles.

His membership in the proletarian cause makes her as happy as a girl. Why?

He arrives. It's seven o'clock at night. There's no union meeting or rally.

Meaningless to be coy.

—Do you want to be my companion, Otavia?

—Yes.

They kiss, suddenly excited.

She undresses, without false modesty. She would give herself to the male chosen by her nature. Purely.

And since that day, they sleep together in the proletarian room.

—Comrades!

Comrade Alfredo is trying to provoke a schism in the

group, we have proof. With his talents he is trying to take charge of the strike movement's leadership. He's a danger! He tends to bossism! We must unmask him. . . Neutralize him! He's a Trotskyite.

Otavia freezes. The accusers point out hard facts. Inconsistencies. Individualism. Errors. They all stare at her, given the concrete evidence. It's true. Alfredo had let himself be dragged into the bourgeois vanguard that disguises itself under the name 'leftist opposition' in proletarian organizations. He's a Trotskyite. He connives and conspires with the most cynical traitors of the social revolution.

The secret committee awaits a word from her.

Her head is resting on her knees. But silence and expectations challenge her.

She rises. Her eyes reflect a pained energy.

—All the comrades know that he is my companion. But if he's a traitor, I will leave him. And I propose his expulsion from our midst!

THE RALLY AT CONCOR-DIA GREEN

The soldiers swell their uniforms and swing their swords on rusty tick-infested hags. Some got drunk with their officers' permission and caracole. They're under orders to trample and kill the unstoppable proletariat. They march in formation toward Concordia Green through the falling night.

—We have neither opinions nor will. They're orders!

—If I were in charge, it's the lieutenant I would trample!

One of them wears a mourning band on his arm.

—My wife's a factory worker. . .

The peanut hawkers gathered.

   —There's going to be a brawl. Let's get out of here.

   —I'm going to hide my basket and come back to watch!

The tragic platoon, steadily, comes closer to the crowd that fills the square. It's headed by an officer who drew his revolver.

   The soldier in mourning is one who goes in the vangard. He keeps seeing his companion appear in front of him in the midst of the impassioned wives. Suddenly he rears his horse, keeps his distance. He draws back . . .

   —My wife is there. Look whom we're going to trample! They're our wives! Our children! Our brothers and sisters!

A stampede to retreat. A tragic young girl collapses in hysterical seizures. The platoon breaks up and slowly encircles the restless crowd. But the invisible police infiltrators mix in the crowd and come close to the giant black who calls to battle by the central bandstand, in a sleeveless shirt. By his side, a proletarian with whip scars on his chest holds up the red flag.

—Soldiers! Don't shoot your own brothers! Turn your arms on the officers . . .

They blasted five times. Running and screaming. The giant falls beside the raised flag.

His enormous body is down. He barely rises to shout while rolling down the steps.

He cries out something that no one hears but all understand. That the fight must continue, whoever falls, whoever dies!

The multitude takes over the square, in a tragic minute expelling deputies, secret agents, horses . . .

They carry him on his back to an automobile.

The police, reinforced, attack with swords and shots.

The red flag drops, hesitates, rises again, drops. To rise again on tomorrow's barricades.

Carlos Marx comes running into the chicken coop in São Jorge Park. And says in the dark to his paralytic grandmother.

—They did to papa just like Rosa Luxemburg!

INDUSTRIAL
RESERVE

Exclusive of vagabonds, criminals, prostitutes, in a word, the 'dangerous' classes . . . — KARL MARX 'Different Forms of the Relative Surplus Population,' *Das Kapital*

Corina awakens to the overgrown and provincial panorama of the festive country house at Penha.

The cold sun highlights her dirty, dreary curls. Her long grey tweed coat's green threads are pulled from wear. Two crimson hearts enliven her pimpled face. The stretched eyes of the ex-seamstress are now distrustful and daring. Her earlier tender impishness disappeared in her ragged eyelashes. Among the new eucalyptus trees she sees new women with purple hands soaping denim uniforms. A little girl with thin legs shows her dirt-covered underpants under a polkadot skirt. Her once proud teeth give a gaping, yellow smile of affection. The young girl runs away. Corina sticks her hands in the vat of suds. Feeling cold, the mulatto straightens her overcoat, pulling the collar up to her nose. She stops to look at the washerwomen working on their haunches and knees.

She never worked again. Whenever hunger strikes she opens her legs for the males. She got out of jail and wanted to make a new life. She looked for work as a maid in the *People's Daily*. She was ready to take on any job for any price. She was always rejected. Once again she gave herself up to prostitution.

Lively little flags. The rustic roof full of life. Restaurant. Corina sits at a stone table on a rough-hewn bench. She suffers from anxiety that goes from her empty stomach to her aching head. She lights the last cigarette from the empty pack that she tears into little colored strips of paper.

—What would you like to order, ma'am?

It's the short fat waiter.

—For now nothing, Paco. I'm waiting for a young man who should be arriving.

Corina isn't waiting for any man. She is waiting for a sandwich. She already tastes the red mortadella with large white eyes in the middle of the warm bun.

The waiter comes by for the fourth time. He notices the

frightened gestures of the seated girl. His squeezes his eyes into a whirl of wrinkles.

—You wait the whole day, ma'am, and he doesn't come.

Corina gets up.

In a swing, a youngster without pants licks the snot from her nose.

—I'll come back tomorrow. If he should come . . . He has a mustache. He's Portuguese but looks Brazilian.

—If you'd like a *pinga* I'll pay for it.

—Would I. . . I'm freezing to death. Look. I can't even pick up my purse.

She shows him her stiff hands.

Ahead a glass case of golden rolls.

—But if you would. . . I prefer bread.

Comforted by the warm alcohol she makes the childishness of her voice and gestures disappear.

She crosses her stockingless legs uninhibitedly, showing little blue spots on her knee. The Italian's wrinkles multiply. From the former attractive Corina, now in rags, her famous legs are still left. They haven't changed. A little thinner but the same bronze tone, well turned, perfect.

The turbulent Tieté. Barges anchored and sailing, full of trunks and heavy men with high-collared shirts the color of cinnamon. The couple finds a place.

The ferry snoring with rusty gears. The cheap cloth of the jacket with a worn lining becomes drenched in the wet underbrush. The black hair curls into hanging vines. Earth, chunks of coal.

Paco roots like a pig in Corina's sterile breasts.

—You're not going to give me anything?

—*Dio cane!* And the bread and the salami and the *pinga*? Do you think your Turkish pipe is worth more?

Night again finds Corina's starving stomach. Sadly she approaches the man on Rangel Pestana Avenue. For her there's only one crisis. The sexual crisis that spreads through the whole worker's district. An old man also unemployed had said to her:

—There's not even anything to eat, my dear. Only if it's out of friendship.

If only she had a decent dress she could dig up someone on São João Avenue.

She heads for the Braz church. She goes in to rest. A thousand candles illuminate the altar covered with gold. She counts them all. On her fingers she counts all the money spent there. How many days she could eat with those wax tongues dripping down the silver candelabra. . .

Many years ago she had sat down on that very bench on a Good Friday, dressed as Magdalene, with the same hair style from Carnival. Her mother, who was young then, earned a lot of money in that house with a garden on Cha-vantes Street.

Contradictory thoughts flood her head drowned in the velvet of the red pew. She spells out the letters on a balustrade.

—Mag-da-le-ne. . .

—Was St. Mary Magdalene ever hungry when she was a whore?

She laughs.

A young priest wrapped in a cassock appears in the round nave. He approaches.

—This pew is reserved. It's forbidden to sit here.

At the door she meets the canon eating peanuts. A beggar's little daughter, chattering, very dark-skinned, in the midst of taxi-stand drivers. Guessing by her breasts, thirteen years old or more. She sells matchboxes.

Corina crosses the street. From the other side she sees a group of youths at a café on the corner. Maybe she can scare up a café au lait.

The whole bar argues heatedly. Corina only sees and smells the encouraging milk and the reheated coffee. A very lively black chewing on a dry corn husk shouts.

Corina hears a friendly voice under a large cap.

—Pepe?

—Damn, Corina! You're a mess.

—Oh, a pigsty! And you? How's Otavia? And the others?

—Don't even mention her!

—Did she dump you?

—Her, nothing doing. I'm the one who lost interest in a kid who puts out for everybody.

The two, clinging together, victims of the same unaware-
ness, cast on the same shore of capitalist ventures, carry
salted popcorn to the same bed.

AFTERWORD

> . . . *na imensa cidade proletária, o Braz*
>
> . . . *in the immense proletarian city, Braz*

Braz, São Paulo, 1890–1933

By 1933 São Paulo was a growing metropolis of a million people. Every fifteen years from the turn of the century, it had doubled its population, marked by waves of immigration that had brought some 200,000 Italians, 25,000 Portuguese, and 5,000 Spaniards in the 1880s alone. Many of these immigrants remained in the city, sometimes outnumbering native Brazilians by a majority of two to one.[1]

The district of Braz, a low area to São Paulo's near east side bordering Avenida Rangel Pestana, connected to town by a streetcar line in 1877, with a rail station and hospice for immigrants, became a commercial and residential center for the working class. The site of large textile factories, Braz was a natural focus of Italian immigration, with a large female working force made up of displaced or marginal persons who moved into subdivided lots and boardinghouses. The district's population doubled to more than 30,000 in the first two years of the 1890s, while Italian became the language of early labor agitation and popular struggle because of the large immigrant labor group, according to Antonio Candido.[2] São Paulo's multilingual environment gave rise to a popular Italo-Paulista dialect with its own press, illustrated by the humorous chronicles of Juó Bananere, circa 1912–14, and documented in the 1920s by the short stories of Antônio de Alcântara Machado and Bananere's comic parodies in *La divina increnca*.[3] By 1925 the textile factories in São Paulo employed nearly 50,000 people, and the value of their products rivaled that of coffee, the basis of Brazil's economy.[4]

The city's growth from 1890 was out of control, dominated by the blind, uncoordinated, and tumultuous pursuit of power and industrialization. Uncontrolled growth in population led to a rapid degeneration of housing, public health, and services. In a speech in Rio de Janeiro's Municipal Theater in March 1919, elder statesman Rui Barbosa (1849–1923) denounced the appalling conditions of the working class and demanded radical reforms (never enacted) to include (1) mandatory insurance, (2) equality of the sexes in work and salary, (3) equal payment of minors according to hours worked, (4) the eight-hour working day, (5) elimination of night work, (6) prohibition of home work, (7) protection of women workers the month before and after giving birth, and (8) abolition of the factory store.[5] Twelve years later Patrícia Galvão, at age twenty-one, chose a dissenting and marginal literary form, the proletarian novel, to promote political change and to document many of the same issues.

Pagu: Revolutionary Muse of Brazilian Modernism

A resident of Braz and student of its Normal School, Patrícia Galvão (1910–62) was a flamboyant writer, artist, intellectual, and militant. She was known after 1928 as simply 'Pagu,' after a poem written about her by Raul Bopp. She had been discovered in the late 1920s by artist Tarsila do Amaral and writer Oswald de Andrade, participants in the modernist period of renovation in national arts and letters. At São Paulo's Dramatic and Musical Conservatory, she studied with Mário de Andrade, whom she called a 'tall and ugly' figure, without knowing of his stature as a poet. Talented and dynamic, Pagu expressed herself through poetry declamation, drawing, and her particular penchant for satire, social criticism, and ideological struggle. When reciting poetry, she added a strong dose of malice to the lyrics. In 1927 she entered a Fox Film beauty contest; her often outrageous dress and makeup showed a taste for mischief, romance, and scandal. Purple lipstick, black eyelashes, and miniskirts shocked her classmates and attracted smart comments, which she answered in kind. It was rumored that she fled from school by going out windows and over walls, wore short hair and transparent blouses, and smoked in public. She constantly questioned and challenged limits, from fashion to politics, forming her own radical critiques of Brazilian intellectuals and society.

Oswald's 'Cannibal Manifesto' of 1928 theorized an aesthetic primitivism for Brazil, in a dialogue with the European vanguards.[6] Pagu's drawings and a poem appeared in the *Revista de Antropofagia*, and she attracted journalist Alvaro Moreyra's attention as 'the girl with crazy hair . . . who abolished the grammar of life. She is the latest product from São Paulo . . . the shining announcement of *Antropofagia*.'[7] In a retrospective account, Pagu asserted that her social novel was related to her participation in the vanguardist aesthetics of the Cannibalist group:

> We've known for a long time what vanguard means. In 1933, we were publishing the first 'social' novel of a 'social' line in S. Paulo, in frank and open language: 'Industrial Park.' Four years before, we had already sided with the 'leftist' and extremist wing of the Cannibal movement.
>
> In such circumstances we desired no other result than what came from taking a position and from research.[8]

The second 'dentition' of the *Revista de Antropofagia* in 1929 supported radical political reforms, including abortion and divorce. Both aesthetic and political features were formative characteristics of *Industrial Park*.

Pagu shared the modernists' avant-garde positions. She traveled to Tarsila's first individual exhibit in Rio de Janeiro in July 1929 and was photographed alongside Anita Malfatti, Benjamin Péret, Elsie Houston, and their circle. When a provocative interviewer asked if she believed in the Cannibalist platform, she answered, 'I don't believe in it; I like it.' Asked if she had books ready to publish, she replied 'Not to publish. My 60 censored poems.'[9] In 1928 Pagu was depicted in a drawing by Emiliano Di Cavalcanti as a large body with a guitar, filling a landscape surrounded by banana leaves, a cactus, and small shacks. The pose immediately suggests comparison with Tarsila's telluric, primitive figure *A Negra,* from her *antropofagia* phase. Pagu's coloristic prose in *Industrial Park* also echoes the paintings of Tarsila—whose ties with the European avant-garde have been well studied[10]—as well as Anita Malfatti's expressionist portraiture. One of Pagu's earliest poems, marked by futurist violence, was written in crayon on a vase in the modernist house designed by Grigori Warchavchik.

Pagu's status as modernist muse culminated in her marriage in 1930 to Oswald, followed by the birth of their son, Rudá de Andrade. Their marriage took place only after an elaborate charade. For the sake of appearances and to disguise their affair, Pagu went through a marriage ceremony with another man, only to be abducted afterward by Oswald, who was waiting on the road to Santos. For a time she lived with him on a small island where he was fleeing creditors. In 1931 she was arrested at a militant rally for Sacco and Vanzetti in Santos, where a black stevedore died in her arms. Traveling to Buenos Aires for poetry declamation, she met the exiled Brazilian Communist leader Luís Carlos Prestes and Argentine writers Jorge Luis Borges and Victoria Ocampo. Back in São Paulo, Pagu authored the radical columns titled 'Woman of the People' for Oswald's short-lived magazine *O Homem do Povo* in March–April 1931. In 1932 she was in Rio de Janeiro living in a workers' district and acting as an armed guard for Party meetings. The Party censured and ultimately expelled her, however, for 'individualistic and sensationalist agitation' and obliged her to use a pseudonym (*mara lobo*) for her proletarian novel, *Industrial Park*.

A nonconformist who opposed Brazil's patriarchal system, Pagu left Oswald and her infant son in 1933 to go to the Orient as a journalist, interviewing Freud en route to China. She sold her interview to a reporter she had met in Hollywood, and her impressions of Freud were lost. From Shanghai and Manchuria she traveled on the Trans-Siberian Railroad to Moscow, where she observed inequities in the Communist system, and went on to Paris, where she studied at the Université Populaire, wrote for *L'Avant-Garde*, and took part in street demonstrations until 1935. The Brazilian ambassador intervened to prevent her deportation to Germany, although the fate awaiting her in Brazil was similarly harsh. Immediately after her return, she was reunited with Rudá and lived for a few short months with him and her sister Sidéria in a small rented room in São Paulo. But the demands of Party militancy led Pagu to return her son to Oswald and his companion Julieta Bárbara, and in time both sisters were arrested. Pagu was jailed for four years as a political prisoner by the Vargas dictatorship and tortured in Rio de Janeiro in the same appalling conditions chronicled by writer Graciliano Ramos in his prison diary from 1937.[11] At her trial by the National Security Tribunal she was described as 'extremely dangerous, very intelligent, speaking diverse languages, an intellectual orator of the red ideology who makes use of printed materials.' Bundles of handbills, stencil paper, a typewriter, a mimeograph machine, a pearl-handled revolver, and the use of the pseudonym 'Pagu' were the main pieces of evidence used to convict her.[12] In 1938 Pagu was visited in prison by Oswald and Rudá, whom she described with pride in a note of thanks as 'chubby, strong, and intelligent.'[13] Her long-awaited release was delayed six months because she refused to greet a visiting politician whom she detested.

Pagu left prison in 1940 in poor health, weighing only ninety-six pounds. At first, for long periods, she refused to speak to anyone. That same year she married art critic and journalist Geraldo Ferraz, who would be her lifelong companion, and her second son, journalist Geraldo Galvão Ferraz, was born in 1946.

Pagu returned to literature through journalism, although her valuable contributions have scarcely been mentioned in literary histories. She published social criticism and personal reflections in a column signed 'Ariel' in the *Diário da Noite* (1942) and continued in 'Local Color' in the *Diário de S. Paulo* (1946); there she also initiated the influential series 'Anthology of Foreign Literature,' which introduced and translated ninety world authors into Portuguese—from Sartre, Camus, and Silone to Hemingway and Faulkner. She herself translated the first excerpt from Joyce's *Ulysses* to appear in Portuguese and was among the earliest reviewers of Fernando Pessoa. In 1945–46 Pagu contributed twenty-four articles to Mário Pedrosa's journal, *Vanguarda Socialista,* which lucidly analyze the lack of direction in national life and values while introducing existentialist ideas. At a national poetry congress she defended the modernist legacy against the new academic poetry of the generation of 1945. Returning to fiction, Pagu coauthored with Ferraz the experimental musical novel *A famosa revista* (The famous magazine), published in 1945—though because of its satirical attack on the Communist party, most prospective publishers found it inconvenient at the end of the war. Poetical and lyrical in style and structure, the novel was intentionally compared by the authors to movements of a symphony. Faithful to her vanguardist training, Pagu once again combined political militancy with experimental poetics.[14]

In the 1950s, Pagu contributed columns of literary criticism and an extended series on Brazilian theater to the Santos daily, *A Tribuna*, in more than 250 literary supplements from 1956 to 1962. She also started a series about television titled 'See? See? See?' Her main interest was contemporary theater, and she translated and produced plays in Santos, including premiers of Octavio Paz, Arrabal, and Ionesco. Her books and translations, donated to the School of Dramatic Art in São Paulo for a library in her name, were unfortunately lost when the school was integrated into the university. Pagu's final personal statement on politics is found in a 1950 pamphlet, *Verdade e liberdade* (Truth and liberty), in which she explained why she became a candidate for the São Paulo state legislature that year.[15] Even after the debilitating years spent under totalitarian ideologies, she retained her faith in bettering society through principles of truth and liberty. Galvão's poetry of social criticism and existential doubt, written under the pseudonym 'Solange Sohl,' remained undiscovered until after her death in 1962, when Ferraz revealed her identity to poet Augusto de Campos. Campos republished selected poems in his extensive anthology of her life and works. Pagu spent her last years, however, struggling with alcoholism and cancer. Near the end she returned to Santos from an unsuccessful operation in Paris, where she had attempted suicide. In a final encounter with the bizarre at her wake, in an atmosphere of passion and heavy drinking, a friend's last embrace tipped over her casket, and her body rolled out onto the floor.

After her death, poet Carlos Drummond de Andrade referred to Patrícia Galvão as the 'tragic muse of the Revolution . . . a woman of great value and sensibility.'[16] In the 1980s Pagu was rediscovered and celebrated in Brazil through films, stage productions, and even cultish emulation in homage to her years of courageous political protest as one of Latin America's most dramatic intellectuals.[17]

Hallucinated City, Industrial Park

Stimulated by contacts with European avant-garde movements and motivated by a desire for national modernization, the strong peripheral artistic and literary movement that developed in São Paulo, in which Pagu later played a part, centered on the 'Week of Modern Art' in February 1922. Young urban artists and writers were encouraged and supported by the landed wealth of the interior coffee aristocracy, whose waning influence no longer sustained its European cultural aspirations and pretensions. The city poet and musician Mário de Andrade, overcome by the commotion of urbanization, composed in a single intense moment of creation the avant-garde poems of his celebrated *Paulicéa desvairada (Hallucinated City)*. In the aggressive 'Ode to the

Bourgeois Gentleman,' Mário attacked the city's bourgeoisie as 'moral mashed potatoes . . . [whose] daughters
play the *Printemps* with their fingernails.'[18] In 1931–32 Pagu
composed an alternate 'hallucinated' narrative document-
ing lives of the city's factory workers in her *Industrial Park,*
published in 1933.[19] Making use of a cinematographic style
of fragmented prose scenes and certainly comparable as an
urban portrait to Mário's poetry, Pagu's novel joined aesthetic experimentation to moral, social, and ideological criticism.

Reflecting the interchange between politics and aesthetics common to the international avant-garde, Galvão
gave shape to the proletarian theme by drawing on modernist techniques. Her expressionistic dramatization of the human costs to the Brazilian industrial system circa 1933 starkly
contrasts the political, economic, and cultural reality of the
immigrant or mulatto labor communities with the city's
elite and its values. By depicting the lower classes in a chron-
icle of city life, Galvão changed the direction of modernist
intellectual and socio-cultural criticism: 'At that time, to
épater, I too wrote my social novel, the first in this city, and it
was called "Industrial Park." All this is history' (*Fanfulla*
12/3/50).[20] Galvão constructed her novel by juxtaposing the
world of labor with the world of capital on every level: statistics of human suffering with industrial statistics; Braz of
female textile workers in the industrial park with salons of
the social elite; the party of the workers with the bourgeois
political parties;[21] Corina's baby deformed by disease with
the legitimated natural sons of society; writings on the wall
of factory latrines with cocktail discourse. Economic ideology is translated throughout the novel into dramatized

scenes of the marginal lives and language of the 'dangerous classes' of vagabonds, immigrants, blacks, and prostitutes who make up the park's industrial reserve.

In a study of Latin American urban labor movements, Thomas Skidmore observes that elite, military, and governmental circles viewed labor organization as a dangerous threat to their interests.[22] After the general strike of July 1917 in Brazil, the union labor movement was subjected to persecution in the form of police repression, imprisonment of 'dangerous individuals,' use of infiltrators, and expulsion of foreign workers as undesirables. A strike in 1919 at the Matarazzo factory in São Paulo, guided by anarchist ideals, was viewed as a threat to the entire social structure, unleashing repression that fell fully on textile workers' strikes in 1920. In 1924, workers' league headquarters were invaded and destroyed by the cavalry. Skidmore nevertheless interprets the confrontation as a sign of the potential power of urban labor. Revolts by dissatisfied army lieutenants who supported a vague platform of national modernization in 1922 and 1924 were not articulated with working-class interests, however, and in effect labor was relegated by elite and ruling interests to recurrent conflict with law and social structure. By the 1930s, writers of the Integralist movement, related to Italian fascism, promoted class hysteria based on the fear of an organized proletarian class. All these tactics are portrayed dramatically in the scenes of *Industrial Park*.

The political militancy of a young female artist with no previously published literary work, however, was complicated by her ties to the iconoclastic 'Cannibal Movement' of 1928. Her denunciation of physical abuse and social injustice was in turn denounced by the city's bourgeoisie and industrial elite classes, to whom the novel was aimed as an outcry. Read neither by the female workers it portrayed, who could not read, nor by the Party, which rejected it because of its implicit anarchism, the novel circulated only among the modernists. The politicization of aesthetics on the theme of labor and syndical organization, as well as the candid language on taboo subjects, placed the work outside the nationalist framework acceptable even to the circles that had supported critical innovation in the arts. Although equal to the radical social criticisms in novels by Oswald de Andrade and Jorge Amado, writers later considered central to nationalist concepts of literary modernism, Pagu's prose passed almost without notice and was not mentioned in any subsequent major history of Brazilian literature. The neglect or exclusion of *Industrial Park* from histories of modernism written since the 1940s and 1950s leaves a conspicuous gap in the definition of the period. Unlike regional works, the urban social novel could not be 'saved' by picturesque description or by the folkloric or indigenous themes then highly valued in the creation of the idea of a national character. The novel's female working-class characters, immigrant dialectal language, and urban geography, alongside its propagandistic political slogans calling for communist revolution, did not at the time fit into accepted theories of either artistic prose, social pamphlet, or national character.

Pagu's rendering of modernist society in fiction and her satirical denunciations of accepted social values were typical of modernist prose that chronicled and parodied city life. Critical viewpoints implicit or latent in the writing of the 1920s, however, became explicit and personified in *Industrial Park*. Such unrelenting, penetrating social criticism could no longer be sponsored or protected by the elite social forces that perhaps paradoxically underwrote Brazil's artistic modernization. Considered taboo, therefore, Pagu's novel, fell out of history. Its position as a 'marginal' work of vanguard forces, however, makes it supremely representative of its modernist moment. Within a retrospective consideration of literary modernism, *Industrial Park* is neither an exception nor a marginal work, but noticeably one of the most forceful, expressive depictions of urban reality within the modernist aesthetic. Its neglect at the hands of literary historians may have affected the novel's status but not its significance. *Industrial Park* is a 'lost' text that alters and enriches our understanding of modernism as a whole. Fortunately, it was reprinted in 1981 on the fiftieth anniversary of its composition.

The novel is both a document and a memoir of the lower depths of the industrial park of Braz, where the author grew up in the 1920s. Names of streets, squares, theaters, and factories become points of reference within a novelistic map of the city. Limousines, trolleys, and cinemas appear as the totems of society's fetish for modernity on the surface of a proletarian world of injustice and suffering. A youthful observer of urban society, Pagu dramatizes contemporary problems of industrialization in the city of São Paulo with camera-eye perceptions of the deep social divisions between elite bourgeoisie and working class that affect the lives of women workers: 'At nine, from the other direction, the luxury train to Rio goes by. The Southern Cross. Each compartment costs four hundred milreis for one night. She earned two hundred a month, sometimes less.'

In Galvão's view, the massive industrial growth statistics,

which she excerpted from a state manual and used as an epigraph to *Industrial Park*, disguise their true costs to the city, which include exacerbated social inequities and human suffering. Political slogans repeated in the novel convey the strict, one-dimensional lines of what passed for political concepts in the period. Marxist criticisms of industrialization drawn from working-class organizations supply both an ideological orientation and raw material for the novel's plot. In her retort to the novel's epigraph, however, Galvão juxtaposed to the industrial data her own invented 'human statistics':

THE STATISTICS AND THE HISTORY OF THE HU-
MAN STRATUM THAT SUSTAINS THE INDUSTRIAL
PARK OF SÃO PAULO AND SPEAKS THE LAN-
GUAGE OF THIS BOOK, CAN BE FOUND, UNDER
THE CAPITALIST REGIME, IN THE JAILS AND IN
THE SLUM HOUSES, IN THE HOSPITALS AND IN
THE MORGUES.

Political and social oppression of workers gives rise to a linguistic and textual depth as the catalyst of 'the language of this book.' Pagu documents an intimate and telling dialect or even ideolect developed by society's 'lower depths' in Braz.

Many issues of the day dramatized by Galvão were denounced nearly four decades later in Warren Dean's classic study of early Brazilian capitalism.[23] The social questions of industrialization raised by Galvão and revived by Dean include starvation wages, long hours, abuse of women and children, accidents, beatings, sickness, and slavery. The '100 streets of Braz' depicted in the novel formed a 'great social penitentiary,' enforced by low wages and long working hours: 'In the city, the theaters are full. The mansions spend on abundant tables. Factory women work for five years to earn the price of a bourgeois dress. They must work their whole lives to buy a cradle.' Galvão openly dramatizes the problems of prostitution, sexual exploitation, racial prejudice, state repression, and economic neocolonialism. Dean notes the Brazilian public's unfavorable opinion of industrialists in the 1920s, stimulated by issues ranging from the inferior quality of products and high prices to such immoral and opportunistic practices as dumping and falsification of labels and patents. In the textile industry of the mid-1920s, the Cia. de Fiação e Tecidos São Carlos showed profits of more than 130 percent per year over invested capital, as did factories in all industrial sectors.[24]

In a recent study of the Paulista textile industry, Maria Alice Rosa Ribeiro corroborates and analyzes the abusive practices prevalent throughout the 1920s. Ribeiro explains how the economic crisis of the 1920s shook the industry through a simultaneous expansion in production and fall in prices, increasing management's desire to maintain price levels by further exploiting the working force, repressing workers' movements, and contravening labor laws and regulations covering salaries and working hours, such as the Holiday Law (1925) and the Code of Minors (1927). Factories were poorly built, crowded with machinery, dark, unventilated, unsanitary, and filled with noxious fumes and chemicals. Workers had to pay for treatment of subsequent illnesses, accidents, or deformities. A system of fines for defects in finished products invariably reduced salaries, already discriminatory by age, sex, skill, and type of product.

Women accounted for 70 percent of the work force, and 38 percent of workers were between eight and fourteen years of age. Managers exercised almost absolute power in the training, supervision, and discipline of the workers, too often shown in violence and abuse against minors, who often worked from five o'clock in the afternoon until six in the morning with only an hour's rest. Ribeiro's study demonstrates how all facets of factory operation contributed to a 'politics of control over the working force.'[25]

Galvão's depiction of scenes from an observed urban social theater of deprivation serves primarily a moral or ethical vision. The author's insights into the city's human dimension accompany the novel's overt political program of social consciousness, reform, or revolution.[26] *Park* denounces the poverty of industrialization in photographic flashes of the lives of female workers in the textile industry at the 'Italo-Brazilian Silk Factory' on Rua Joly, and the oppressive social, sexual, cultural, and industrial environment. Her eye for detail in montage in scenes at the factory gates could be compared to Eisenstein's filmic treatment of revolution. The author's underlying purpose is to dramatize individual tragic circumstances in the lives of the immigrant community as critical examples of the human dimension of Brazil's uncontrolled industrial development before 1930.

Industrial Park is divided into sixteen titled chapters, better characterized as dramatic scenes or vignettes, which combine to form a social mural. Each chapter is composed of a number of interior scenes, identified in the text only by spatial separations, that add to the variety of experience within the literary social theater. The novel as a whole contains 124 such interior scenes, in which slices of life are conveyed with cinematographic force. The novel as a structure may be either read as a linear accumulation of scenes, amounting to the chronological accumulation of episodes in Galvão's social mural or theater, or viewed as an album of photographs, independent camera-eye documents of experience. The chapters are linked through the lives of the book's main characters, the social milieu, geographical landmarks, and the workers' growing movement toward revolution.

Park represents the confluence of commitment to both art and politics characterizing vanguardist fiction.[27] Positions and values explicit in manifestos and journals of the 1920s came to the test with the socioeconomic crisis of 1930. Jorge Amado, in a preface to his first novel, *País do Carnaval* (dated December 1930), characterized the moment as one of struggle and failure: 'This book is an outcry. Almost a call for help. Here is a whole dissatisfied generation that is searching for a purpose . . . fighting against doubt.'[28] Galvão's composition develops from two sides of personal experience: fascination with the experimental poetics of modernist prose, and residence in Braz. Stylistic lines of cinematographic, fragmentary, and documentary images conveyed in plastic-synthetic language and syntax are joined to a proletarian theme and the political program of her 'Woman of the People.' It seems clear that the aggressive harmony inherent in the novel's stark juxtaposition of the two different worlds of elite and working class (also the structural basis of *País do Carnaval*) in fact extends the social criticism and parody characterizing earlier modernist prose works, likewise based on portraits of modernist society, to include a broader depiction of life in the proletarian working classes.[29] The startling mixture of modernist poetics and social dramatization constitutes a form of literary expressionism found widely in this period. Characterized by the 'velocity, strong colors, and personality' perceived in 1933 by critic Ary Pavão and directly comparable to Di Cavalcanti's paintings of the period, Galvão's representation of reality is colored by an expressive fragmentary, cinematographic prose communicating her artistic vision of characters, events, and ideological conflicts. *Industrial Park* unites modernist simplicity with expressionist techniques and ideological positions.

Galvão's novel can be differentiated from contemporary works by social realists because of her penchant for parody and satire conveyed with detached, ironic humor. Her ready-made title, for example, is lifted from billboard advertisements on the electric streetcars of the São Paulo Light Company, which proclaimed: 'São Paulo is the greatest industrial park in South America.' Proletarian passengers refer to the small trolleys that carry them to work as 'imperialist shrimp.' Readers are left wondering on the first page what a 'passing shrimp' could be, constituting proof that the novel was intended for a coterie that 'speaks the language of this book,' as the author states in the epigraph. The juxtaposition of the city's two social worlds, one high and the other low, is approached mainly through satire. Factory women's work on the looms is the subject of ivory tower poets of the protected classes: 'In the salons of the rich, lackey poets declaim:—How beautiful is thy loom!' The decadence of the elite is telegraphed in striking juxtapositions: 'Automobile Club. Inside flies.' The parody is intensified because many of her characters and scenes are drawn from recognizable participants in São Paulo's modernist artistic circles of the 1920s. The resulting prose both satirizes and documents the city's social milieu, extending from its elite to the working class and referring to both modernization and industrialization.

Primitivism in the Park: 'Corrosive Beauty'

In one of the few contemporary reviews, Ary Pavão cited as responsible for the work's artistic force the notable simplicity with which it portrays the human and social inequalities of class society: 'Fleeting novel, primary colors, personality . . . read with pleasure. Improper for minors and ladies—like all books containing ideas—it interests us because it portrays with notable simplicity the most desolate aspects of the tremendous struggle that human inequalities brought about in the different social layers.'[30] Influenced by the intentional stylistic simplicity of modernist texts of the 1920s, Pagu added ideological colors and tones that Pavão associated with 'the violence and brilliance of her revolutionary temperament' to achieve a text marked by social and aesthetic primitivism.

Reread today, *Park* retains the historical force of its primary colors, reductionist social portraits, and rhetorical formulas. The simplicity of the novel's design is the literary equivalent of canvases by modernist artist Tarsila do Amaral in the mid-1920s. Both are related to the precepts of Oswald de Andrade's 'Manifesto of Brazilwood Poetry' of 1924 in its primitivist, geometrical definition of the Brazilian nature and landscape, 'savage and our own.'[31] A Brazilian disciple of Fernand Léger, Tarsila applied primitivist constructionism and primary colors to portray Brazilian society in her Brazilwood phase. Themes in *Morro da Favela, São Paulo (135831),* and *São Paulo (Gazo)* (all from 1924) express the innocence of poverty with simple icons of industrialization and strong, rudimentary colors, which Pagu would recapitulate in her scenes of São Paulo's industrial park in 1931–32. What Geraldo Ferraz criticized as a certain rudimentariness in the 1933 novels of Galvão and Jorge Amado (*Cacau*)—visible in the use of political slogans, the rigid portrayal of character types, and present-tense narration, for example— is an aesthetic quality, paralleling developments in the plastic arts, that contributes to the novel's strong color, symbolism, and expressionism. In 1933 João Ribeiro registered a similar judgment in a review: 'The truth is that the book will have countless readers because of the corrosive beauty of its living paintings of dissolution and death.'[32]

Pagu's portrait of the São Paulo working class bears striking similarities to Eric Hobsbawm's description of archaic forms of urban social movements.[33] Her preindustrial Brazilian workers had not been born into a world of capitalism but were first-generation immigrants who clashed with a revolutionary system they did not understand. In their labor organizing and protest rallies they correspond to Hobsbawm's reformist group of urban poor who, lacking any specific ideology, riot or rebel against the rich and powerful without seeking to overthrow the social order. Though Braz's workers were open to ideological indoctrination— precisely the role of Rosinha and Otavia—their revolutionary potential remained 'primitive,' in Hobsbawm's terms, because of its inherent idealization of anarchic rebellion. An impassioned worker in the protesting mob shouts, 'Soldiers! Don't shoot your own brothers! Turn your arms on the officers.' The novel's grounding in anarchical syndicalism outweighs its projection of Party ideology.

Candido reminds us that during the early decades of the twentieth century, socialism and anarchism presupposed an overriding belief in the revolutionary capacity of knowledge and art to transform and humanize society. The militants of these two perspectives, composed largely of Italians, fought for reduced working hours and improved conditions in the factories. A manifesto by seamstresses could well come from a chapter of *Industrial Park*:

> We also want some free time to dedicate a few hours to reading, to study, because we have very little instruction; and if this situation continues, we will always remain simple, unaware human machines, manipulated at will by the most guilty assassins and thieves.
>
> How can we ever read a book when we leave for work at 7 in the morning and return home at 11 at night? Of the 24 hours, we have only 8 left for rest, not even enough for sleep to replenish our exhausted energies! We have no horizons, or better, we have a dark horizon: we are born to be exploited and to die in the darkness like brutes.[34]

Founded in 1900, the Lega Democratica Italiana supported a workers' movement, as did the Centro Socialista Internacional (1902), which continued to publish the first socialist newspaper in Italian in São Paulo, *Avanti!* (begun in 1896). In the early years of the century, workers' presses featured titles such as *O amigo do povo, La battaglia, Folha do povo, O grito operário,* and *A luta proletária,* while the journals *A plebe* and *A classe operária* represented workers' aspirations in the 1920s. In the latter journal (July 1925) São Paulo textile workers listed their complaints as lack of work, half as much salary for women as for men, exploitation of child labor, oppression in the workplace, and cancellation of bonuses. Their platform called for an eight-hour day, no layoffs, equal wages, the right to organize and to publish a newspaper without persecution, hygienic facilities, and factory space for a workers' school.[35] In a pamphlet distributed to textile workers in 1931, the year Patrícia Galvão began her novel, the principal calls were for the restitution of a 30–40 percent salary cut, a general increase in salaries, fifteen days' vacation, increased pay for work increased from two to six looms, payment for overtime, more than three days' work per week, suspension of fines for defects discovered in the woven cloth, and the end to expulsion and imprisonment of workers who protested.[36] The reformist beliefs and revolutionary militancy of workers' groups, notwithstanding their working conditions, were sufficient to characterize them as groups marginal to Paulista cultural norms.

Galvão's purposefully rudimentary approach to characterization and theme, rejecting the standards of psychological complexity associated with the realist novel, belongs to the primitivist aesthetic common to vanguard movements, sharpened in the *Revista de Antropofagia*. Within the primitivist metaphor, the depiction of the mulatto seamstress Corina and her co-workers, for example, reproduces Di Cavalcanti's colorful, expressive portraits of mulatto women (*Cariocas,* 1926). On a larger scale, her literary social mural, depicting a political rally at Concordia Green, for example, is faithful to the spirit of Cândido Portinari's scenes of the poor, suffering classes in Brazil of the 1930s, while rendering precisely the actual conditions of the working class in the textile industry of Braz. The primary, or primitivist, nature of social portraiture in the plastic arts finds a strong parallel in the characters and ideology of *Industrial Park*.

Another dimension of the work, perhaps not fully apparent to the reader, is Patrícia Galvão's critique of Brazil's modernist movement on the level of allusion. Her own participation in modernist circles and salons allowed the young Normal School muse to contrast life in the industrial park with the social habits and mentality of Brazil's intellectual and cultural elite, years before her marriage to Oswald de Andrade. In Galvão's double life, as in the novel, working-class neighborhoods coexisted with intimate scenes of elite Brazilian intellectual and social life drawn from modernism's first phase. Galvão applied her penetrating wit to the perceived decadence of this elite class—portrayed in soirées, garçonnières, hotels, and clubs—contributing in the novel to a broader criticism of the modernist program of 1922 through parody. Galvão leads the reader inside socialite Dona Olivia Guedes Penteado's modernist salon on Rua Conselheiro Nébias, the meeting place of young artists and the social elite, through a series of devastating portraits of people and events she witnessed around 1929:

> The bourgeoisie plan mediocre romances. Jokes ooze from the depths of the cushions. Caviar is crushed by filled teeth. . . Dona Finoca, old patroness of new arts, suffers the courting of a half-dozen novices. . . The garçonnière has a number of antique and futurist rarities. . . A sexual desperation of separation and ruin is in the air. The bourgeoisie entertains itself.

D. Olivia's large salon, decorated with works of modern art (Picasso, Léger, Tarsila, Di Cavalcanti, Gomide, Malfatti, Segall, and so on) and a grand piano, provided the modernists with a venue for their works and ideas in the company of Brazil's elite.

The novel as history and social document is matched by an uncanny series of presentiments. Otavia, patterned after Patrícia Galvão, becomes a political prisoner at the Dois Rios Colony in the novel; the author herself would spend four years in the political prisons Maria Zélia and Paraíso (São Paulo), the Detention House (Rio de Janeiro), and the Public Jail (São Paulo). Rosinha Lituana, expelled from Brazil, predicts the fate of Olga Benario,[37] wife of Luís Carlos Prestes, who was deported to Nazi Germany in 1936:

> In the interrogation, they tell her they're going to expel her.
>
> —You're a foreigner!
>
> But she's never known another country. She had always given her labor to Brazil's rich!
>
> She smiles bitterly. They're going to take her away from Braz forever. . . What does it matter? She had heard it from the very defenders of the social penitentiary:—Poor people have no country!

Alexandre's call for a political party of the workers, antithetical to Party directives, preceded by forty-five years the organization of the PT (Partido dos Trabalhadores) in São Paulo in 1978 by Luiz Inácio da Silva (Lula), a candidate for the presidency of Brazil in 1989: 'What party should we support, comrades? The parties of the bourgeoisie? No! The P.R.P or P.D.? No! The lieutenants? No! All workers must come into the Party of the workers!' Otavia's rejection of Alfredo at the insistence of Party officials, despite her own desires, predicts Pagu's own separation from Oswald in December 1933: 'All the comrades know that he is my companion. But if he's a traitor, I will leave him. And I propose his expulsion from our midst!' According to Antônio Risério, Pagu's injection of ideology into vanguardist literary techniques anticipates Oswald de Andrade's political novels—*A Escada Vermelha, Marco Zero*—and his theater of the 1930s.[38] The novel also foreshadows the future schism between Brazil's intellectuals and the Communist Party— unexpectedly the subject of Galvão's second novel, *A famosa revista*—through the unorthodox viewpoints and 'deviations' of the characters Rosinha Lituana, Alexandre, and Alfredo.

The scope of Galvão's social world is indicated by the fifty-two characters named in her relatively short novel. The lives of the main characters are intertwined with the issues and personages of a wide, contradictory social world. The first major character introduced is Rosinha Lituana, an organizer for the Brazilian Communist Party created in homage to Rosa Luxemburg,[39] while strangely reminiscent of Olga Benario.[40] Alexandre, the giant black labor organizer at Concordia Green, is patterned after the dockworker Herculano de Souza, who died in Pagu's arms at the Sacco-Vanzetti rally. Other characters depict São Paulo's modernist world of artists, authors, immigrants, and nascent industries.

In 1933, Pavão considered the connections between fictional characters and reality to be obvious: 'Otavia, Alfredo and Eleonora—the main characters in the novel—everyone can recognize. The first two are walking about, happy with the ideals they embraced.' Eleonora, in fact, combines a miscellany of attributes of the women associated with Oswald de Andrade,[41]—from 'Deisi,' modernist muse of the garçonnière whom he married *in extremis* in 1919, to the artist Tarsila do Amaral, married to Oswald 1926–30, to Pagu herself: 'Eleonora is boarded sexually by her fiancé Alfredo before marriage and lives by reciting at parties. Patrícia Galvão, when she married Belisário, was expecting a child by Oswald and declaimed poetry in meetings of the *cannibal* group. . . . Eleonora is a student at the Braz Normal School. Patrícia Galvão, as we have seen, studied at that School from 1924 to 1928, when she made her first contacts with Oswald de Andrade.'[42]

Alfredo Rocha is a critical but sympathetic characterization of modernist author and intellectual Oswald de Andrade. The only male character developed in the novel, Rocha is one of the few fictional views of this important modernist intellectual. He appears as a 'vacillating bourgeois' headed toward socialist transformation while reading Marx in the comfort of the Hotel Esplanada. After he and Eleonora meet in Braz, the couple attends a soirée offered by Dona Finoca, after which Alfredo resigns from the bourgeoisie: 'I hate these people. These parasites. . . And I am one of them!' Rocha, unlike Eleonora, agonizes over his wealth and identity, exercising his doubts when Otavia appears at the Esplanada to deliver three dresses:

—Do you think that I want to abuse a worker? You're mistaken. Personally you don't interest me. . . It's your class. . .

—Of course! We're the ones who give you this luxury!

—You're mistaken. . . This comfort is a burden to me.

Within the 'isolating walls' of social elite circles, Rocha is increasingly alienated by his feelings of uselessness and tries to join the working class with his new-found Marxism: 'Alfredo tries to like the shabby and poorly prepared food. He feels happy. He doesn't find Brazil abhorrent, as before. He doesn't need to drown his individualistic irritability in any native picturesque. Without longing for the hotels of Cairo or French wines.' Yet he is expelled from the Party for 'unresolvable deviations.' The denunciation can be compared with interest to the self-criticism of Oswald's alter ego, the character Jorge D'Alvelos, in his novel *A Escada* (1934):

> He intended to improve, in an emotive and sensational discovery; now he searched out places he had disdained in his cretinous aristocracy as an artist. . . . His adhesion to Marxism could not dissimulate the passionate side in all his endeavors. That's the way he was, the way he had been brought up. The only way he sincerely could have joined antiromantic socialism, calculating and constructive. Romantically. . .[43]

Otavia, who accompanies Rosinha Lituana in ideological commitment and social action, is the author's self-portrait, one whose tragic, uncanny premonitions certainly exceeded the bounds of Galvão's conscious imagination. Her self-portrait may also be compared to D'Alvelos's description of her as the character Mongol who led him to Marxism in *A Escada:*

Could she be the companion he needed? The one promised him by all the poorly understood effusiveness? Was it she? . . .

He needed a sentimental revindication. With this complete, free woman to rebuild his life, now consciously. For the first time someone had told him that there was a world, the organized country of all those who had revolted, of all the oppressed, of all those condemned by bourgeois society. There was a world capable of justifying the protests of his life.[44]

Other characters parody well-known figures: Count Sgrimis, the 'Green Count,' unites Count Francisco Matarazzo, owner of São Paulo's 'Industrias Reunidas,' with visiting German social philosopher Count Herman Keyserling. Eleonora is forced to recite verses of the conservative Paulista poet 'Pirotti Laqua' (Menotti del Picchia) and accompanies Alfredo to the modernist salon of Dona Finoca, 'old patroness of new arts,' a transparent critical allusion to D. Olivia, the wealthy aristocrat who feted a circle of young artists.

In addition to the other named characters, Galvão introduces a gallery of social types, identified mainly by occupation, amounting to more than eighty persons. From elite modernist salons, the reader is carried into the commotion of São Paulo streets. Issues of class, race, and working conditions are raised by the novel's characters in a sequence of scenes. Corina, for example, trapped in her job for long hours, agonizes over the problem of race: 'Why had she been born mulatto? And so pretty! . . . The damn problem is her color. Why that difference from other women?' Rosinha Lituana, committed to ideological indoctrination, explains the mechanism of capitalistic exploitation to factory workers who organize in a syndicalist meeting with its cross section of working society. Union members protest poor working conditions and long hours. The unemployed are marching in the streets for bread and jobs.

Many of the themes and viewpoints in *Industrial Park* are drawn from the author's experience as a woman of twenty-one. For example, class distinction applies to the way women are treated in the 'birthing houses': 'The little children of the paying class stay close to their mothers. The indigents prepare their children for the future separation demanded by work. The bourgeois children are nurtured from early on, linked by the economic umbilical cord.' Galvão never considers herself to be a feminist, however, and parodies the supposedly emancipated, intellectual women of São Paulo. Scenes document the triviality and dependency of these liberated daughters of the bourgeoisie with whom modernists socialized:

—My maid delayed me. With excuses of pregnancy. Dizziness. She made my bath too cold.

The German *garçon,* tall and thin, freshens the cocktails. . . . The sharpened tongue of the little virgin absorbs the crystal cherry. . . . The Paulista Educational Radio vomits foxtrots off the wall.

When suffrage is obtained for women (1932), Pagu notes that working women are excluded because of illiteracy.

A critique of eroticism and sexism in Brazilian society is central to the novel, which openly treats subjects considered as strictly taboo, such as masturbation, lesbianism, prostitution, venereal disease, and rape: 'At Carnival I'm going to Braz. . . . Girls throw themselves like cats clawing the ser-

pentine streamers. Their sexes are burning. . . . The bourgeois go by in their cars, agreeing that Braz is good at Carnival. . . . In Braz the bourgeoisie search for new and fresh
meat.' Taboo social practices are viewed in the light of class
function. Corina, contemplating suicide on the Viaduto do
Chá after her infant son's death, accepts prostitution as the
only solution for her poverty. Pagu denounces wives of the
rural aristocracy as contraband brought to Brazil by a corrupt organization, 'Zwi Migdal,' that furnished unsuspect-
ing Polish immigrants to Brazilian prostitution rings. She
notes that the aristocracy has only legitimate sons, even
though eroticism pervades the whole of society:

—Some women do it with women.
—I don't believe it. They can't.
—Yes they can. I read it in a book.

The exemplary woman in *Park* is Rosinha, who struggles
to raise the social consciousness of factory women and works
toward what she sees as a better world, yet the mulatto Corina's suffering is more central to the novel as drama and social
manifesto. Her problems, those of Braz itself—hunger, poverty, exploitation, and discrimination—overshadow and sub-
sume sexual themes. In the final chapter Corina takes her
place in a proletariat become vagabonds, criminals, and
prostitutes marginalized by the industrial machine.

'Living paintings of dissolution and death'

Pagu's novel can be placed within a negative dynamics of
the avant-garde that favors a state of permanent revolt. *Industrial Park* constitutes yet another 'necrology of the bour-

geoisie,' comparable to Oswald de Andrade's label for his novel-invention *Serafim Ponte Grande* (1933). The negative dialectics of the industrial park, counterposed to progressive notions of machines and modernization, lies in its inventory of superfluous lives and infernal underworlds of industrial society in the boardinghouses, factories, and streets of Braz. In her dual labor as worker and mother, for example, Corina is both sensuous and diseased; society denies her healthy offspring while preparing her body for prostitution. Matilde, from the poor quarter of Braz, is seduced by the decadent Eleonora in the elite and modern hotel Esplanada. Congruent to the body's role as object of occult desire, selected emblems of the modern age—limousines, trolleys, billboards—become totems for the urge to subordinate and dehumanize the urban masses, exposing the photographic negative of their modernizing image. Although the novel parodies elite locales, from Madame's fashion atelier to the Esplanada Hotel, such worlds nonetheless represent prohibitions to the workers; any attempt to cross their borders, outside the confines of subordinate labor, is a transgression. The function of violation is to translate story or event into pathology and, finally, necrology: the factory gate, the final whistle, an abandoned slipper. Revolution, as well, is a fatal transgression of the borders between opposing social worlds. A function of Pagu's use of language as transgression is to challenge those who would 'put the revolution in quotation marks.'

Cannibalism is the metaphor Pagu applies to social and industrial bodies. It is another of the negative structures cultivated within the novel's state of permanent contradiction: incorporation versus exclusion, liberty versus subjugation, syndicate and neighborhood versus nation. The negativity of the text finally resides in the dissolution of the icons of modernity—from cinemas to factories to bodies—into symbolic forms of historical, social, or political decay: 'the pale enigma of Greta Garbo, in the poorly drawn colors of a poster. Disarrayed hair. Bitter smile. A prostitute feeding the imperialist pimp of America to distract the masses.' The death of the industrial present is disguised in a poetic, frag- mented style of vivid expressionism. One of the occult themes underlying such a design is redemption—the mu- latto worker Corina's fundamental urge to live—which Pagu pursues through her linguistic power of invocation, the book's 'frank and open language.' The death of modern- ist language, however, is also a function of its tabooed body. Pagu's linguistic portrait thus concludes on the tragic level of Corina's condemned life.

The Poverty of Industrialization

Historian E. Bradford Burns questions whether modern- ization in Latin America may have caused more harm than good.[45] A growing export economy may have been illusory, reinforcing the negative effects of such colonial social insti- tutions as the latifundia while threatening an indigenous ecological and agrarian system that supplied the needs of lo- cal consumption. In Burns's view, growth and moderniza- tion do not necessarily lead to development; he questions whether the elite desired more than surface modernization without reform of institutions, since little benefit accrued to the impoverished majority in educational, health, or labor conditions. Poverty through progress is his reading of the

South American industrial park. Pagu's novel is an expressionist portrait of the human cost of industrialization in São Paulo. Vividly colored by the linguistic and social emblems of its place and age, it documents the lives of women workers and the coming of age of the exploited laboring class. Mara Lobo, an alter ego reminiscent of Herman Hesse's in *Steppenwolf* (1927), parodies and criticizes bourgeois society and its values, while advocating radical political and economic as well as humanistic alternatives. The novel is also an insider's accusation of hypocrisy and irresponsible wealth against Brazil's social and industrial aristocracy, depicted through the very elite modernist circles that the author frequented and drafted in the language of Braz's underworld. By widening the scope of satirical and critical modernist social portraiture, *Industrial Park* projects vanguardist poetics into a proletarian world. The dramatic, expressionistic result is a human, social theater of labor in which the actors' lament echoes from the 1930s to the present:

> Other men will remain. Other women will remain.
> Braz of Brazil. Braz of the world.

NOTES

1. Richard Morse, *Formação histórica de São Paulo* (São Paulo: DIFEL, 1970); rev. trans. of *From Community to Metropolis* (Gainesville: University of Florida Press, 1958).

2. Antonio Candido, *Teresina etc.* (Rio de Janeiro: Paz e Terra, 1980), 48.

3. Antônio de Alcântara Machado, *Brás, Bexiga e Barra Funda* (São Paulo: Hélio, 1927), *Laranja da China* (São Paulo: Gráfica Editora,

1928), and *Mana Maria e vários contos* (Rio de Janeiro: José Oympio, 1936); Alexandre Ribeiro Marcondes Machado (pseud. Juó Bananere), *La divina increnca* (São Paulo: Irmãos Marrano Editôres, 1924; rpt. São Paulo: Folco Masucci, 1966).

4. Edgard Carone, *O P.C.B. 1922–1943* (São Paulo: DIFEL, 1982), 134.

5. Rui Barbosa's speech is excerpted in Paulo Pinheiro and Michael Hall, *A classe operária no Brasil* (São Paulo: Brasiliense, 1981), 2:271–84. Pinheiro and Hall also document Italian women textile workers in São Paulo in photographs from the 1920s.

6. Oswald de Andrade, 'Manifesto Antropófago,' in *Do Pau-Brasil à antropofagia e às utopias* (Rio de Janeiro: Civilização Brasileira, 1972), 11–19; trans. as 'Cannibal Manifesto' by Leslie Bary, *Latin American Literary Review* 19.38 (1991): 35–47.

7. Quoted in Augusto de Campos, *Pagu-Vida-Obra* (São Paulo: Brasiliense, 1982), 323.

8. Patrícia Galvão, 'Neoconcretismo,' *A Tribuna* (Santos), sup. 107 (12 April 1959): 4. All translations are mine unless otherwise noted.

9. Quoted in Campos, *Pagu*, 323.

10. Aracy Amaral, *Tarsila, sua obra e seu tempo,* 2 vols. (São Paulo: Perspectiva/USP, 1975).

11. Graciliano Ramos, *Memórias do cárcere,* 4 vols. (Rio de Janeiro: José Olympio, 1953).

12. I obtained National Security Tribunal documents on the prosecution of Galvão in 1937, containing this passage, from the Brazilian National Archive.

13. Quoted in Campos, *Pagu*, 330.

14. Patrícia Galvão and Geraldo Ferraz, *A famosa revista* (Rio de Janeiro: Améric-Edit., 1945).

15. Patrícia Galvão, *Verdade e liberdade* (São Paulo: Edição do Comité Pró-Candidatura Patrícia Galvão, 1950).

16. Carlos Drummond de Andrade, 'Imagens de Perda: Patrícia e João Dornas,' *Correio da Manhã* (Rio de Janeiro), 16 January 1963.

17. Important sources about Patrícia Galvão include Brazilian poet Augusto de Campos's comprehensive, annotated anthology on her life and works, *Pagu-Vida-Obra,* and Geraldo Ferraz's memoirs, *Depois de tudo* (Rio de Janeiro: Paz e Terra; São Paulo: Secretaria Municipal de Cultura, 1983). Actress Norma Benguell played Pagu in the film *Eternamente, Pagu,* inspired by Campos's book and by documentaries such as Ivo Branco's *'eh! Pagu eh!'* In academic circles, there is a master's thesis by Aldo Luis Bellagamba Colesanti, *'Parque Industrial:* Ideologia e Forma' (São José do Rio Preto–UNESP, 1984), excerpted in his article 'O romance 'Parque Industrial' de Patrícia Galvão: Um estilo de confluência,' in *Letras & Letras* (Revista do Departamento de Letras da Universidade Federal de Uberlândia) 1.2 (1985): 3–16. For critical surveys in English of Pagu's life and ideas, see Susan K. Besse, 'Pagu: Patrícia Galvão—Rebel,' in *The Human Condition in Latin America,* ed. William H. Beezley and Judith Ewell (Wilmington, Del.: Scholarly Resources, 1987), 103–17; and Jayne Bloch, 'Patrícia Galvão: The Struggle against Conformity,' *Latin American Literary Review* 14.27 (1986): 188–201. On *Industrial Park,* see also K. David Jackson, 'Patrícia Galvão and Brazilian Social Realism of the 1930's,' *Proceedings of the Pacific Northwest Council on Foreign Langauge* 28, pt.1 (1977): 95–98.

18. Mário de Andrade, *Paulicéa desvairada* (São Paulo: Casa Ma-

yença, 1922); trans. as *Hallucinated City* by Jack E. Tomlins (Nashville: Vanderbilt University Press, 1968).

19. *Parque Industrial* (São Paulo: Edição do Autor, 1933) 2d ed., São Paulo: Alternativa, 1981). This unusual work by a woman of twenty-three who raised a dissenting voice within the São Paulo group of modernist artists is mentioned only briefly in the *Dicionário de autores paulistas* by Luís Correa de Melo and merely listed in Galvão's second novel, *A famosa revista,* coauthored in 1945 with the modernist journalist and art critic Geraldo Ferraz, whom she married in 1940. An early review was published in 1933 by Ary Pavão in *Bronzes e plumas* (Rio de Janeiro: Renascença, 1933); and João Ribeiro praised it in a 1933 review republished in his book *Crítica-os modernos* (Rio de Janeiro: Academia Brasileira de Letras, 1952), 337–39. In 1977 this early social realist novel could not be found in any public library outside of São Paulo, however, and was largely unknown until its second edition in 1981.

20. Patrícia Galvão in the São Paulo magazine *Fanfulla*, December 3, 1950. Antônio de Alcântara Machado's *Brás, Bexiga e Barra Funda* (1927) is subtitled 'Notícias de São Paulo,' and Plínio Salgado's *O Extrangeiro* (1926) carries the subtitle 'Chronica da Vida Paulista.' Oswald de Andrade's *A Trilogia do Exílio: Os Condemnados* (1922) and Mário de Andrade's *Paulicéa desvairada* (1922) are also works tied to city life.

21. The two parties mentioned in the novel are the Partido Republicano Paulista (P.R.P.), the Republican Party of São Paulo; and the Partido Democrático (P.D.), or Democratic Party.

22. Thomas Skidmore, 'Workers and Soldiers: Urban Labor Movements and Elite Responses in Twentieth-Century Latin America,' in *Elites, Masses, and Modernization in Latin America*,

1850–1930, ed. Virginia Bernhard (Austin: University of Texas Press, 1979).

23. Warren Dean, *The Industrialization of São Paulo,* Institute of Latin American Studies, Latin American Monographs No.17 (Austin: University of Texas Press, 1969).

24. Carone, *O P.C.B.,* 314.

25. Maria Alice Rosa Ribeiro, *Condições de trabalho na indústria têxtil paulista (1870–1930)* (São Paulo: HUCITEC/UNICAMP, 1988): 186–93. Other recent studies of the Brazilian textile industry include Stanley J. Stein, *Origens e evolução da indústria têxtil no Brasil, 1850–1950* (Rio de Janeiro: Campus, 1979); Luiz Pereira, *Trabalho e desenvolvimento no Brasil* (São Paulo: DIFEL, 1965); and Vera M. Cândido Pereira, *O coração da fábrica: Estudo de caso entre operários têxteis* (Rio de Janeiro: Campus, 1979).

26. While there were many international examples of literary works, grounded in the naturalist school, that denounced the problems, abuses, and adverse consequences of industrialization, as well as an incipient anarchist movement in Brazil before 1920, there was obviously a strongly utopian character to Galvão's literary project, considering the highly limited and elitist nature of Brazil's readers of fiction.

27. Art and politics in vanguard prose is discussed in Charles Russell, *Poets, Prophets, and Revolutionaries* (New York: Oxford University Press, 1985).

28. Jorge Amado, *País do Carnaval* (Rio de Janeiro: Editora Schmidt, 1931), 'Explicação.'

29. In an earlier study I suggested that the dialectic of ideology and aesthetics defines the novel by carrying over the aestheticism of literature and politics of the 1920s to the politicization of culture in

the 1930s (Jackson, 'Patrícia Galvão and Brazilian Social Realism of the 1930s'). Although from that perspective *Industrial Park* can be defined as a hybrid work that bridges both decades, ultimately the accepted classification of modernism into decades is artificial and unproductive.

30. Pavão, *Bronzes e plumas,* 20–22.

31. Oswald de Andrade, 'Manifesto da poesia pau Brasil,' in *Do Pau-Brasil,* 3–10; trans. as 'Manifesto of Brazilwood Poetry' by Stella da Sá Rego, *Latin American Literary Review* 14.27 (1986): 184–87.

32. Geraldo Ferraz, *Depois de tudo;* João Ribeiro, *Crítica-Os Modernos,* 339.

33. Eric Hobsbawm, 'The City Mob,' in *Primitive Rebels* (New York: Praeger, 1963), 108–25.

34. Quoted in Edgard Carone, *O movimento operário no Brasil (1877–1944)* (São Paulo: DIFEL, 1979), 471.

35. Cited in Pinheiro and Hall, *A classe operária no Brasil,* 127–30.

36. See Carone, *O P.C.B.,* 318–19.

37. See Fernando Morais, *Olga* (São Paulo: Alfa-Omega, 1986).

38. Antônio Risério, 'Pagu: Vida-Obra, Obravida, Vida,' in Campos, *Pagu,* 18–29.

39. Rosa Luxemburg (1871–1919) was one of the founders of the Polish Socialist Party (1892) and after 1898 a leader of the German Social Democratic Party. A participant in the revolution of 1905 in Russian Poland, she later formed the Spartacus Party in Germany during World War I, which after 1918 became the German Communist Party. She was killed by soldiers in January 1919. See *New Co-*

lumbia Encyclopedia (New York: Columbia University Press, 1975), 1633.

40. Olga Benario Prestes (1908–42), present in Germany in 1919 and later married to Luís Carlos Prestes, was deported in 1936 (while seven months pregnant) from Brazil to Germany, where she died in a concentration camp in 1942. Her story is told in Morais, *Olga.*

41. For further information, consult Maria Augusta Fonseca Abramo, *Oswald de Andrade, 1890–1954: Biografia* (São Paulo: Art Editora/Secretaria de Estado da Cultura, 1990).

42. Colesanti, *'Parque Industrial:* Ideologia e Forma,' 29–30.

43. Oswald de Andrade, *A Escada* (São Paulo: Global, 1991), 64–65; first published as *A Escada Vermelha* (São Paulo: Companhia Editora Nacional, 1934).

44. Oswald de Andrade, *A Escada,* 57–58.

45. E. Bradford Burns, *The Poverty of Progress: Latin America in the Nineteenth Century* (Berkeley: University of California Press, 1980).

Volumes in the *Latin American Women Writers* series include:

The Youngest Doll By Rosario Ferré. Introduction by Jean Franco

Mean Woman By Alicia Borinsky. Translated by Cola Franzen

P

Industrial Park was set on
a Linotron 100 machine, in
Matthew Carter's Galliard
types. Stencil, keyed on the
Macintosh, was used in the
display matter. The text was
composed by Kim Essman.
Design by R. H. Eckersley.

CPSIA information can be obtained
at www.ICGtesting.com
Printed in the USA
LVHW051117250821
696066LV00006B/967

9 780803 270411